W9-DHL-961

THE FARM MYSTERY SERIES:

MIDNIGHT SKY

By Mr. and Mrs. Stephen B. Castleberry

Castleberry Farms Press

All rights reserved, including the right to reproduce this book or portions thereof, in any form, without written permission from the authors.

This is a work of fiction. All the characters and events portrayed in this book (with the exception of the organization Voice of the Martyrs) are fictitious, and any resemblance to real people or events is purely coincidental.

All scripture references are from the King James Version of the Bible.

First Edition
© Copyright 1998

ISBN 1-891907-06-9

Castleberry Farms Press
P.O. Box 337
Poplar, WI 54864

Printed in the U.S.A.

Cover art was created by:
Jeffrey T. Larson
11947 E. State Rd. 13
Maple, Wisconsin 54854

Chapter One

Andy tossed and turned in bed. For some reason he couldn't seem to sleep. Drowsily, he rubbed his eyes. *I wonder what woke me up?* he thought. He looked over at his brothers, both of whom were snoring gently.

"Bark! Bark, bark, bark, bark! Bark! Bark, bark, bark, bark!"

Now, I remember. Andy lay there trying to figure it out. *Whose dog can that be? It sounds like it's close to the house.* He thought of all the dogs in the neighborhood. No, this dog didn't sound like any of the neighbor's dogs.

Andy got out of bed and looked out the window. It was a very dark night. Occasionally a flash of lightning would fill the sky with a brilliant light, revealing billowing layers of dark, angry-looking clouds. Glancing at the clock in his room, he noticed it was 12:01. "Midnight," he muttered to himself, crawling back into bed.

"Bark! Bark, bark, bark, bark!" Over and over the dog continued to noisily make his presence known. It was always a single bark, then a slight pause followed by four rapid barks.

Andy was about to get up and look out the window when he heard the front door open. He lay very still, listening.

"Get out of here! Go on, dog! You're going to wake the whole house up!" Dad was obviously annoyed at the dog, and his tone of voice showed it. Even though Dad was trying to shout "quietly," Andy noticed that both brothers, Jason and Ben, started stirring as Dad addressed the dog.

"Bark! Bark, bark, bark, bark!" Dad's commands seemed to have had no effect on the dog.

Silently, Andy slipped out of bed and quietly descended the stairs. He walked up right behind his dad who was looking out the front window. Dad seemed so intent on looking that Andy hated to say anything. So he didn't. Instead he got closer and tried to see what Dad was looking at outside.

"Bark! Bark, bark, bark, bark!" Dad suddenly spun around toward the door and ran right into Andy before seeing him in the darkened house.

"Oop . . . !" Dad sputtered, as the two fell to the floor. "Who are you?" Dad demanded. The room was very dark.

"I'm Andy, Dad!"

Dad immediately apologized. "I'm sorry! Are you all right, son?" When Andy assured him that he was okay, he continued. "What are you doing sneaking up on me like that, not making a sound?"

"I'm sorry, Dad, but I wasn't trying to sneak up on you," Andy replied. "You looked so busy watching out the window that I didn't want to interrupt you."

Dad gave a long sigh, then apologized again. "Any idea whose dog that is out there, serenading a family that doesn't want to be serenaded?"

Andy moved to the window and looked out. Dad had flipped on the switch so the front yard was bathed in light. It was pouring down rain. The gutters were having such a hard time with the heavy spring rains that several waterfalls were running over the sides. "What a messy night!" Andy exclaimed. Then he saw the dog. It was a short, black dog with long curly hair hiding its eyes.

"Bark! Bark, bark, bark, bark!"

"No sir," Andy finally said. "I've never seen that dog before. I know all the dogs around here, but I've never seen him before."

"Me, either," Dad agreed. "What I can't figure out is why he just insists on standing outside our door and barking. I've tried to scare him away, but it didn't work. He acted like he wanted to come in!"

Now Dad and Andy were both staring out the window at the dog. He noticed them, and tail wagging, he walked over to the front door, as if expecting to be let in. The dog looked from the front door over to the window where Dad and Andy were looking out. "It looks like he's saying, 'Okay, enough fun now, it's raining out here. Let me back in!'"

"I'll try once more to get him to go home," Dad said, moving toward the front door.

"Dad . . ." Andy spoke a little hesitantly. "Dad, you may want to shout a little quieter this time."

Dad laughed. "You're right! Here I am trying to get the dog to go away so we can get some sleep, and in the process, I am probably just waking up the rest of the household." So instead of shouting he walked to the front door and opened it a crack. The sound of the rain was almost deafening. "Go on home!" Dad said in a whispered 'shout.' "Go on!"

The dog seemed to love this attention and tried to

3

squeeze through the narrow crack offered by the door. Dad shut the door some more to keep the dog from coming in. "Go on!" he said one more time. However, it was obvious that either the dog didn't understand Dad or had no intention of obeying. With tail wagging briskly, the dog whined and tried to push his nose through the doorway.

Dad closed the door and walked to the basement. He came back with his tall mud boots on, opened the front door and then closed it behind him.

Andy raced to the window and couldn't help but laugh. Dad looked so funny with his pajamas and mud boots on, chasing the dog in the pouring down rain. He didn't even have an umbrella to keep him dry.

Dad kept running toward the dog, which caused the dog to run toward the road. But when Dad started walking back toward the house, the dog followed right behind him, tail wagging happily. After a few attempts, Dad raced back to the house, flung open the door, and stepped inside. The dog tried to come in, but Dad closed the door before he could.

Andy laughed out loud. There stood Dad, water dripping from his hair, his pajamas soaked with rain. Dad, however, didn't seem to be in a laughing mood. "It's late, Andy. Time to get back in bed. We'll have to see about the dog tomorrow, if he's still here." It was clear to Andy that Dad didn't intend to talk about this any more tonight.

Andy slowly walked back to his bed, trying his best not laugh again. That was hard to do. Dad's boots squeaked as he walked down the stairs to the basement.

As Andy tucked himself into bed, his mind was

whirling. *Whose dog is that? Why does it think it's supposed to come into our house? And why won't it stop barking?* Andy thought some more. *What if the dog's master is out there somewhere in the rain, maybe even hurt? What if the dog was trying to get them to come to his master's rescue?* Andy had read about such things happening before. He started to get out of bed and tell his dad about this possibility. No, it was obvious that Dad didn't want Andy to get out of bed again. Besides, Dad had probably already thought of that.

Andy was awake a long time. Finally, however, sleep began to overtake the tired boy. Just as he was about to go to sleep, the dog let him know that it was still there. "Bark! Bark, bark, bark, bark!" *What's going on?* Andy thought. *Maybe this will be something The Great Detective Agency can look into tomorrow. Sure, it will be the Case of the Unknown Dog.* With that thought, he finally dropped off to sleep.

Chapter Two

Andy, are you going to sleep all day?" It was Jason, Andy's twelve-year-old brother, calling to him the next morning.

Ten-year-old Andy slowly rolled over, looked at Jason with half-closed eyes to avoid the light streaming in the window, then rolled back over.

The sound of a little boy giggling filled the bedroom. That distinctive sound could only come from one person: Andy's six-year-old brother Ben. "Did you see how he looked at you?" Ben asked Jason, still giggling.

Andy lifted one eyelid and looked at the clock by his bed. *It can't be that late*, he thought. Saturday morning was beginning earlier than usual. At least it seemed to him that it was.

Jason and Ben continued to get dressed for the day while Andy lay motionless on his bed. "I smell sweet rolls," Jason coaxed, with emphasis on the word 'sweet.' "Mmm, don't they smell good, Ben?"

This was too much for Andy. Struggling, he lifted his head. "I'm getting up, guys. Don't eat them all," he said hoarsely, as his brothers left the bedroom to head down to breakfast. *Surely they won't eat them all*, he thought, flopping his legs over the side of the bed. *Mom wouldn't let them.* But a boy who is still half-asleep, after being up in the middle of the night, doesn't always think straight. *I better get down there quickly*!

Squinting to avoid the light coming in through the window, Andy slowly rose to his feet and moved toward his closet. Moving around helped to wake him up, and before long he was putting on his favorite pair of jeans and his blue plaid shirt. He wasn't only dressing, however. He was also thinking. Thinking about what happened last night. The Case of the Unknown Dog was coming back to him. *I'm sure that Jason doesn't know anything about it*, he thought, dressing as quickly as he could. He wanted to be able to help Dad tell the story at the breakfast table of what happened last night.

Before long, he was entering the kitchen. Mom smiled at him and handed him a glass of juice. "Good morning, Andy. I wasn't going to get you up yet, after you were up so late last night. How do you feel this morning?"

The aroma of the sweet rolls was overwhelming. "I feel fine," Andy admitted. "Just hungry! And a little tired."

After the blessing, the food was passed. "What happened last night?" asked fifteen-year-old Cathy, handing him the plate of sweet rolls. "I remember it raining awfully hard sometime during the night."

As Cathy asked that question, Andy had just popped a huge bite of sweet roll into his mouth. He wanted to tell the exciting story of the dog, so Andy tried swallowing the food in his mouth quickly. It didn't work well. Andy got choked and started coughing.

"Are you all right?" Mom asked. Andy nodded,

but continued to cough. "Don't take such a big bite, Andy," cautioned Mom with concern. "And chew your food before swallowing."

If nothing else, at least the choking prevented any more conversation about the dog until Andy was back to normal.

When Andy regained his ability to speak, he started telling about the exploits of the night before. "I'm tired this morning, because Dad and I were up last night trying to scare away a dog that wouldn't leave. Actually, Dad did the work. I was just up watching."

"Whose dog was it?" asked Cathy. "Now that you mention it, I remember hearing a dog bark and bark."

"So do I," echoed Jason. "But I didn't feel like getting out of bed and seeing whose dog it was."

"We don't know, do we, Dad?" Andy stated in the form of a question. Andy hoped to tell about the dog, but wanted to let Dad tell the story if he wanted to.

"No, I've never seen the dog before," Dad agreed. He knew Andy would enjoy telling the story, and asked him to continue.

"It's a short black dog with real long, curly hair. You know, one of those kinds that has so much hair that you can't see their eyes. It kept barking and acting like it wanted to get in the house."

"Was it a mean dog?" asked Ben, frightened. He could picture a dog trying to get in and bite someone.

"No, he seemed very friendly," Andy responded. "His tail never did stop wagging, even though it was pouring down rain."

Andy just had to stop talking for a minute and eat a bite of his delicious sweet roll. While he did so, the questions came streaming from Ben and Jason.

"How did you try chasing him away, Dad?" Ben asked. "Did he run away when you chased him?"

Dad looked a little vexed, recalling the incident. "Hardly! Every time I ran toward him, he would bolt. But just as soon as I turned around to head back to the house, the dog followed, tail wagging like I was his best friend and was just playing with him. Finally, I had enough and gave up."

Andy started laughing. He had suddenly remembered what his dad looked like when he reentered the house after this ordeal.

"What's funny?" Jason asked.

Dad grinned. "Go ahead, Andy. Tell them the whole tale! I'm fine now."

Andy laughed again. "Dad went outside and chased the dog in the rain. I mean it was pouring down. He was wearing his tall mud boots. And he didn't even have an umbrella! When he came in, the water was running over his nose like a faucet and his pajamas looked like they had just come out of the washing machine." Ben, Jason, and Cathy laughed.

Mom looked concerned. "Did you change your pajamas, honey?"

Everyone laughed.

"Well, if you didn't chase the dog away, where did it go?" asked Jason, who was rising from his seat as he asked this question. "I wonder if he's still out there?" By now he had reached the back door next to the kitchen and was looking out. "No dog here."

"He was by the front door last night," Andy said,

getting up to look. Ben was already moving to the front door, and opened it wide. Then he shut it quickly.

"There's a dog out there!" he exclaimed.

"Let me see!" Jason said with excitement. He flung back open the door to get a good look. The dog looked in at the three boys, and with tail wagging, trotted briskly into the house.

Chapter Three

Hold on there, boys!" Mom directed, coming from the kitchen. "No dogs allowed! Not in the house, anyway."

"Come on, boy." Andy coaxed the dog back outdoors. The dog seemed reluctant to follow, but then Andy offered him a piece of his sweet roll, which he had brought with him from the table, and the dog followed the sweet smell back out into the warm spring sunshine. The Nelsons lived on a small farm, nestled near the mountains of southeastern Tennessee, and this time of the year was absolutely delightful.

Three excited boys followed the dog outside but Mom gave different instructions. "You guys need to come in and finish your breakfast first. Then you can look at the dog."

"Yes ma'am," Ben replied, leading the group back to the table.

"Looks like a case for The Great Detective Agency, partner!" Jason was glad to have a new mystery.

"Agreed, partner," Andy answered. The boys had formed a detective agency a few years ago to solve the mysteries that occurred on the Nelson farmstead. Although they were just boys, they had some measure of success in solving mysteries and helping get needed information. Their office was located under the basement stairs, which provided a somewhat cramped but secluded place to conduct important business. When they weren't homeschooling, doing chores, or outside playing, they could often be found there, sifting through clues and determining their next course of action for a case. The Nelson family members didn't hesitate to 'hire' the boys to solve mysteries. Not only were the boys good at what they did, they were also free.

After breakfast, Jason asked if they could look at the dog before doing chores. Mom agreed and the boys raced to the front door. Sure enough, there was the dog, tail wagging, waiting for the rest of his sweet roll.

Daylight revealed a slightly different dog than Andy remembered from the night before. The color of the hair was actually grey, not black, with a tint of blue in it. It was a short dog with lots of life and vitality. Also, Andy noted that it looked very well fed and cared for. Its shiny coat had obviously been clipped recently. The result was a dog that looked well-groomed, except, in Andy's opinion, for the bunch of hair covering the dog's eyes. Apparently the storm the night before had been responsible for the animal's muddy condition, and Andy suspected that this dog didn't often look dirty.

"Hello, boy!" Jason petted the blue-grey mass of hair, and combed it with his hands to the side. "Do you have any eyes in there?"

"He has eyes and he has a collar, also," Andy informed. "And the collar has a phone number on it!"

"Great!" Jason responded. "Let's see what it says. 'Mountain View Veterinary Clinic, 3914 E. Pinedale Road, (615) 443-3298, 0023898.' And this other tag says that he got his rabies shot this year. Well, it looks like the mystery is solved almost before we have even started on it."

"I suspect all we have to do is call that phone number, give them the dog's ID number, and they will tell us who the owner is," Andy agreed, sounding disappointed. "I was hoping that we would have a new mystery to solve."

"Me too," Jason said. "Well, let's go do our chores and then we can call this clinic."

The boys walked to the barn, and the dog must have felt it had some chores to do also because it followed along with them, tail wagging with every step.

After chores, the boys asked permission to call the clinic. "I don't think it will be open today because it's Saturday, but I'll try." Mom didn't quite understand why this information brought happy faces to the boys. She was soon back in the living room. "They are closed today. Unless of course, you have an emergency, in which case they offer an answering service's number you can call. This isn't an emergency, though."

"Don't call them, Mom," Jason said. "We would hate to bother the vet on his day off! Besides, maybe we can find the owner ourselves."

"How kind of you boys," said Mom, laughing. "Another mystery for The Great Detective Agency?"

"Yes ma'am," Andy said. "We'll try to solve it for you, don't worry."

"Thanks, guys," Mom answered. "I know that whoever lost their dog is probably missing it by now."

Jason thought as he walked out of the living

room. "We need a plan of action," he stated. "Let's head to our office and think this case through some."

Soon they were seated in their tiny office, a flashlight trying to remove some of the darkness that enveloped the "room."

"Let's write down some of the clues that we have. You know, some of the things that we know about the Case of the Unknown Dog," Jason began. As president of the agency, he usually started the official meeting in the office.

After much discussion and thinking, the following list was compiled in little spiral notebooks that each member of The Great Detective Agency carried to record clues about mysteries.

1. Dog arrived Friday night, about midnight. Maybe a little sooner.
2. It was raining hard when dog arrived.
3. Dog seems friendly, like someone has taken care of it.
4. Dog has tag: Mountain View Veterinary Clinic, number 0023898.
5. Dog refuses to leave our farm. Reason unknown.

"Let's see. Number 6. Dog is a . . . Hey, I just realized that we don't know what breed of dog it is," Jason remarked. "That could come in handy today."

"I'll run and get the 'D' encyclopedia and bring it down," Andy offered. It took a long time for Andy to return and his brother was about to go and check on him when Andy's footsteps sounded on the basement steps right above Jason's head. Dust floated down into Jason's hair and onto his open notebook. It was one of the inconveniences of having an office under the stairs.

"Sorry it took so long," Andy apologized. "But I couldn't find the 'D' encyclopedia for a long time. It was under your desk with three straws, a cork, and a coat hanger on top of it."

"Oh, I forgot," Jason explained. "I was doing some research on dams. I'm going to build a model dam! It will have a real turbine, just like some dams do that make electricity. And it's going to have some irrigation pipes; that's what the straws are for. It's going to be neat!" Then Jason remembered the subject at hand. "Well, at least you finally found the encyclopedia."

"Yes, but it didn't help anyway," Andy said. "It had pictures of lots of kinds of dogs. Jason, you just wouldn't believe how many different kinds of dogs there are! There's this one dog that sometimes only weighs one pound. Can you believe that? It's called a Chihuahua and the little thing is only about five inches tall," he related, picking up a ruler and holding it up to see how small that would really be. He whistled low. "Guess what they used to be called? 'Pillow dogs,' because people let them sleep inside their pillows to keep them warm. Can you believe it?" Now Andy realized that he, too, was getting sidetracked. "Anyway, the picture of our unknown dog wasn't in there."

"Too bad," Jason started, but Andy interrupted.

"Which is why I asked Cathy if she knew where any more pictures of dogs were. At first she said 'no,' but then remembered that we had an old book on dogs in the bookcase. That took us some time to find, and then when we did find it, the pictures were spread throughout the book instead of being in one place."

"Did you ever find it?" Jason was getting a little exasperated with Andy's detailed account. If the truth were told, Jason was mostly annoyed that he hadn't accompanied Andy on this short expedition upstairs. It sounded like it had been fun.

"Yes, and it's a Kerry Blue Terrier," Andy replied, reading from notes in his spiral notebook. "They originated in Ireland sometime in the 1800's and average between thirty and forty pounds."

Jason wrote these facts in his notebook.

"Now what?" Andy asked.

"I suppose the most obvious thing to do is to check with our neighbors to see if they have gotten a dog recently that we don't know about," Jason answered. The boys had already brain stormed, trying to think of whose dog this could be, without success.

"Let's see if Mom will let us ride our bikes to some neighbors' houses," Andy suggested. "It might end up being that easy."

"Good plan," Jason agreed. "Of course, we have to keep open the other possibilities."

"Like what?" questioned Andy.

"Well, someone might be hiking or camping around here and had this dog with them. Then they got separated somehow."

"That's true," Andy nodded. "But wouldn't they come looking for it? Hey, you know what we should do?" Andy had a sudden inspiration. "We should put a sign on our mailbox that says 'Dog found. Inquire within.'"

"Another good idea," Jason agreed, writing this in his notebook. "Now, what other explanations could there be?"

Both boys thought. "I hate to say it, but it could be that someone just dumped their dog off and drove away," Andy said sadly. "It seems hard to believe, but people do it. Especially people from the city. They just figure that a dog can survive in the country."

"I hope that's not what happened with this dog," Jason responded. "Seems like too nice of a dog to me."

"Well, let's keep that as a possibility, anyway. I didn't say I wanted it to be true, but we can't just ignore possibilities because we aren't fond of them," Andy reminded his brother. "So, should we make that sign and see if we can go to our neighbors?"

The boys hand-painted a sign and placed it below their mailbox, tied on with baling twine. It read "Dog found!!" Jason had decided, and Andy finally agreed, that "inquire within" sounded too formal for a sign tied to a mailbox out in the country.

"Let's go get permission to ride our bikes to the neighbors!" Andy said. "Maybe they know something." With that, the boys raced to the house.

Chapter Four

Mom gave them permission to check with their neighbors, but said it had to be done quickly. Mom and Dad were packing their suitcases for an important trip that was to begin on Monday. They had been praying for some time that God would open the door for them to adopt a child from another country. With God's blessing, the home study and other adoption processes had gone unusually smoothly. Now Mr. and Mrs. Nelson were packing to fly to Russia to pick up two children to adopt.

The boys first rode their bikes to Mr. Cartwright's house. Mr. Cartwright, their closest neighbor, was a bachelor in his 80's. Andy knocked on the door and stepped back. Both boys waited politely for a few minutes. Nothing happened. Jason stepped forward and knocked again, a little more loudly this time. Sometimes Mr. Cartwright didn't hear so well. Still no answer. "Guess he's not home," Jason commented as he wrote a short note to place on his door.

"Maybe he's out looking for his new dog that is lost!" Andy suggested.

"Could be," Jason replied. "I know he didn't used to have a dog like that, but you never know when someone is going to buy something new. Still, it doesn't quite seem like Mr. Cartwright to buy a dog, somehow."

Midnight Sky

The boys jumped on their bikes and rode to another neighbor's farm. This was the Claymore Farm, a small dairy that milked sheep and sold the milk to a special creamery for making cheeses.

Mrs. Claymore answered the knock right away. "Good morning, boys. How are you?" Then noticing an excitement in Andy's countenance, she added, "Is everything okay at your farm?"

"Yes ma'am," Andy replied. He liked Mrs. Claymore, because she seemed fond of young boys and almost always had a cookie or treat to give them. "We found a dog and we're trying to see if you know who the owner is."

Mrs. Claymore laughed. "No new dogs here, boys. The five we have are plenty, I'd say. I'm not complaining though. We really need every one of those dogs to protect the sheep." She thought a minute, while her fingers tapped her lips. "What kind of a dog is it?"

Jason described the dog, and as he finished, Mrs. Claymore smiled as though she knew a secret. "I know someone who has a dog that sounds like your lost dog. Dave Smith just got a dog that looks like that. Hasn't had him long, I don't think. I haven't actually seen him up close, just from the road as I drive by. But I wouldn't be surprised if that's your dog owner!"

"Thanks!" Andy said. "We'll go see if the Smiths are at home right now."

Mrs. Claymore turned to go back inside. "Wait a minute, boys. Here, have a piece of fudge. It just came out of the refrigerator where I was getting it hard."

19

Jason looked at Andy, who just looked at the fudge longingly. "Thank you, Mrs. Claymore. I . . . I . . ." Jason was having trouble making himself say what he felt he should say. "I'm afraid it might mess up our lunch if we ate it right now."

"How silly of me," Mrs. Claymore responded. "Of course, you're right." She then disappeared into the house and the door closed behind her.

The boys were walking away when the door swung open again. "Here, I wrapped it in a piece of plastic. That way you can have it after lunch. I put a piece in for Ben, too."

"Thanks!" Andy smiled, gratefully.

I sure like Mrs. Claymore, Andy reflected as they turned their bikes toward the road. *When I get old and have a house of my own, I'm always going to have boxes of candy and treats to hand out to children when they come to my house*, Andy thought. *And for me, too!*

It was a beautiful, warm morning with birds singing. The boys seemed to be engrossed in thought and didn't talk. How good Andy felt and how much energy he had. Mom always said that boys feel better and stay healthy more if they eat good food. He also remembered what Mom had said about boys that didn't eat things that were good for them, and the diseases and behavior problems they had. Andy was glad that Mom was a good cook and that she knew the kinds of foods that made boys really feel good. He started wondering what they were having for lunch. Before long, his stomach felt empty. *I sure hope it's not long before we eat*, he thought, looking at the position of the sun in the sky. *Maybe not too long*, he hoped.

Then Andy looked down in his bike basket at the package of fudge. Mmm, it sure smelled good. Yet, something didn't seem quite right. What was it? Andy thought back over things. Mom certainly let her family have sweets sometimes, so that wasn't the problem. Then what was? Finally, he remembered his unspoken resolve to give children lots of candy when he was a man who owned his own house. *Maybe I'll give away fruit or raisins instead,* he thought. Yes, that made more sense. Feeling like he was making a better decision, even though it would be years before he could implement it, Andy rode on with a clear conscience.

As they neared the bend close to the Smiths' house, Jason broke the silence. "Maybe we're close to solving the Case of the Unknown Dog. I'm glad, of course. But I was hoping that we could call the vet on Monday and then track down the owner that way."

"At least maybe we'll finally get some of our questions answered," Andy said. "What I still want to figure out is why the dog came to our house? And why does it act like it lives at our house? It starts to walk inside every time we even crack the door open."

"I know what you mean," Jason agreed. "The dog seems to think we're its owners and always have been. Most dogs act a little bit shy of you at first. At least they don't act like you're their owner or something."

Their conversation ended as they pulled into the Smiths' driveway. Riding their bikes near the back door, they got off and started walking toward the house. "Bark! Bark, bark! Bark!" A dog inside the house must have seen the boys.

"Doesn't sound like Mr. Smith has a lost dog to me," Andy noted, walking closer toward the glass storm door. A black dog with long hair suddenly appeared in the doorway and barked through the glass. Andy wasn't sure if the dog was glad to see them or not. He took a step back.

Jason seemed a little cautious himself. "Should I knock, or what?" he asked.

"I don't think you have to knock," Andy said loudly in order to be heard over the barking dog. "I would think that if anyone is home they know that someone is here!"

Sure enough, Mrs. Smith could be seen approaching the door. She was hobbling and leaning on a crutch. She struggled to get the dog to move back so she could get to the door, but the dog had other ideas. He continued to bark. Finally, she dropped her crutch, put a hand on the door frame to support herself, and grabbed the dog's collar with the other hand. She then motioned for Andy to open the door, an act that she was incapable of doing given her limit of two hands.

Andy reluctantly opened the door a bit. Sure, she had hold of the dog, but what if he broke away from her? Such wasn't out of the question, given Mrs. Smith's rather precarious position.

"I'm sorry to bother you, Mrs. Smith," he began. "We found a dog and were wondering if you had lost one or knew of someone who had."

The dog began barking again just as soon as Andy started speaking. Mrs. Smith talked to the dog, and tried shaking him a little to make him stop barking. Finally, she said with exasperation, "Just a minute, boys." She then picked up her crutch and painstakingly pulled the still-barking dog out of the room.

"I don't think she's going to be able to help us," Jason confided. "I wish we hadn't bothered her. I wonder why she's on crutches?" This was a mystery, but not the kind the boys were allowed to work on.

"I know. But we can't leave now. We have to wait until she comes back," Andy reminded. His stomach was now positively growling.

In several minutes, Mrs. Smith returned to the door, hobbling slower than she had previously. She opened the door and invited the boys inside.

"No thank you," Andy answered politely. He wasn't going into that house with that dog inside there somewhere. "Again, we're sorry to bother you. We found a dog and we're trying to see if you have lost one," he stated concisely. He didn't want to take up more of her time than absolutely necessary.

"No, but sometimes I wouldn't mind losing one!" Mrs. Smith laughed, looking in the direction she had pulled the dog. She then explained to the boys that her dog was a gift from her father, who had wanted to give her a dog to cheer her up after her surgery. "I have to admit, boys, the dog isn't cheering me up much. At first we had him outside, because Dave, I mean Mr. Smith, doesn't like inside dogs. But Roger, that's the dog's name, howled so much to be let in that we finally broke down and let him inside. He's been better since he's inside, although you wouldn't think it right now. He was an inside dog at Father's house. His biggest problem seems to be strangers. He just can't seem to stop barking when a stranger comes into the yard." A dog started barking somewhere in the house and Mrs. Smith looked worriedly over her shoulder. "Oh, that Roger! I hope he's not standing on the couch again!"

"We'll let you go," Jason offered. "I hope your dog works out for you, Mrs. Smith. Have a nice day."

"Goodbye, boys," Mrs. Smith said. "And if I hear of anyone who has lost a dog I'll let you know." The sound of Roger barking more loudly caused Mrs. Smith to suddenly turn and hobble back into her house. "Now, Roger, if you're on that couch again . . ." Mrs. Smith's words became hopelessly lost in the noise of Roger's constant barking.

"We haven't solved the mystery," Jason remarked, getting onto his bike. "Let's go home and get some lunch. Maybe we will think of something else that will give us new clues."

"Great idea!" enthused Andy. The boys raced home on their bikes and arrived just as Mom was setting the table. The smell of homemade bread and a pumpkin pie filled the air. Andy looked at the package of fudge and placed it on the kitchen counter. Mom could do with it as she liked. He didn't think anything could taste as good as Mom's bread with sweet honey.

Chapter Five

After a time of prayer, the meal began. "Well, have you made good progress in packing, honey?" Dad asked Mom.

Mom seemed a little nervous. "I don't know! I mean, yes, I've got most things packed that we can pack already. But I've never packed for a trip to Russia before. I don't know for sure what we will need and what things we definitely don't need."

"What about the list that the adoption agency gave us? Does that help?"

"Somewhat," Mom said. "But it says that the weather can be unpredictable. Although it's supposed to be getting warmer, like here, it can suddenly get cold or rainy or anything. It doesn't help that we aren't allowed many pounds for our luggage."

"I understand," Dad said, soothingly. "And it's not like we can just drive to a store over there and buy what we want. Well, we will just have to do the best we know how and then trust that God will bless our efforts."

"When will you be leaving on the plane?" Ben asked. This was not the first time this question had been raised, and was the second time Ben himself had raised it today.

Dad was patient. "We will fly out on Monday evening at 8:30. Remember how Grandad is going to be taking care of you? We'll be gone for several weeks and then when we return, we'll be a big happy family of eight! Won't that be great?"

"Yes!" Ben answered, cheerfully. It was still somewhat hard to believe that what Mom and Dad had been praying about for years was finally going to happen.

"Is there anything else we can do to help you get ready?" Cathy asked. "I would be happy to help you pack, but I wouldn't know what to put in."

"I'm not sure you could do worse than me!" Mom exclaimed. "Thanks, but I am feeling a little less stressed after what I've gotten done this morning. If I can think of anything, I'll let you know."

"Of course, the best thing you can do for us is to pray for us," added Dad. "Pray for our safety and that the adoption would go smoothly in Russia. Things can come up at the last minute while we're over there. But if you remain faithful in praying for us, you'll be praying for us even in those rough times. We want God's will to be done, that's all."

"Honey, you wanted me to remind you about you-know-what," Mom said, speaking to Dad softly, with a meaningful glance at the top of the refrigerator.

"Oh, thanks!" Dad responded. "I've been busy this morning too, and I forgot to tell you about it last night when I got home from work." He walked over to the refrigerator and pulled down an envelope. "The guys at the mill gave this to me yesterday at lunch." Dad worked at a local lumber mill, where he drove a fork lift loading logs onto the conveyor and moving finished lumber around the yard.

Pulling out the card, Dad began to read.

Midnight Sky

"Timothy,

It's not often that someone we know does something really, really good. Your willingness to adopt some children with health problems from Russia is outstanding. Thanks for giving us an example of the kinds of stuff we should be doing. And thanks for being our friend. Hope all goes well for you in Russia.

P. S. And remember, don't drink the water!

It's signed by most of the workers at the mill."

"That's nice," Cathy said. "I mean that it's nice that they took the time to pass a card around for everyone to sign."

Mom smiled, but tears began to form in her eyes. "That's not all they did," Dad continued, smiling. "They also took up a sort of collection to help with some of the adoption expenses. As you know, since you've seen us watch our money very closely this last year, adopting a child from Russia is very expensive. Well, I guess the guys figured that out somehow. Anyway, they gave me a check for $750."

"Wow!" Andy exclaimed. "Are you going to keep it?"

"Given the spirit it was offered in, and that we've been praying for God to open up doors for this adoption, yes, I'm going to keep it. To be honest, we were wondering how a few bills were going to be paid. There have been some unexpected costs that came up recently, and we were sort of struggling. This is God's provision. We had no idea how we could get the money, but here it is. God is so good."

"Does God always make sure someone gives you money?" Ben asked, munching on another piece of bread and strawberry jam.

"No," Dad admitted. "Sometimes He doesn't do anything like that at all. God didn't promise that He would give us everything we wanted. Just that He would give us everything we needed. My mother's favorite verse was Philippians 4:19 which says 'But my God shall supply all your need according to his riches in glory by Christ Jesus'."

"But you needed the money," Ben objected.

"Yes, in the way we think of things on earth, we needed the money. But God says that the only thing we **really** need is Him. In the book of Colossians we are told, ' For in him dwelleth all the fulness of the Godhead bodily. And ye are complete in him . . .' So you see, we are actually complete in Jesus, which means that being a Christian is all we **really** need. I thank Him that He has met that need. And no one can take it away from us, either."

Everyone let that lesson sink in a bit. Then Dad asked, "What are you children going to do this afternoon?" Cathy said that she hoped to work in the garden, while the boys didn't have any definite plans beyond afternoon chores.

"How much more do you have to do, Connie?"

"I'm really close," Mom responded. "I would say that I should be finished with everything I could do today in about an hour. Why?"

"Oh, I was thinking that especially since we're going to be apart as a family for a while, that we might do something fun. How about a bike ride on the road at the foot of the mountain?" That was the children's favorite place to ride bikes. However, since the bikes had to be loaded and hauled to ride there, most rides were usually much more local in nature.

Everyone was excited by the prospects of Dad's suggestion and worked hard to get ready for the happy excursion. The afternoon was passed in pleasure and a renewed gratefulness for God's provisions. His provisions for the beautiful world He created, as well as His provisions of creating a family that loved each other so much.

That night after Bible reading and prayer, the boys lay down in their beds after kissing their parents goodnight. Looking at their still-excited faces, Mom said they might talk quietly for a few minutes, as long as they stayed in bed and didn't get wild.

"This was a fun day," Ben sighed with contentment. "I love to ride bikes on that zooming-down hill!"

"It was great!" Andy agreed. "And we got to work on a mystery, too. Have you thought any more about it?"

"Some," Jason replied. "It seems that we have exhausted most avenues we can take. We've put up a sign on the mailbox and we've checked with the neighbors. I guess our next step is to call the vet on Monday and see who the owner is."

"Yes," Andy agreed. "But even if we do find the owner, that still won't answer some questions I have. Like why the dog seems to think we're his owners. And why he showed up at our house in the middle of the night last night in that bad storm. And why, if someone has lost him, they haven't come by to find him yet."

"Those are good questions, Andy," Jason agreed. "Maybe the owner will tell us if we can find him."

"Maybe," Andy mused. "I think I'm going to try to think of the answers, though, before the owner tells us." With that the boys settled down and before long, were fast asleep.

Chapter Six

Monday was a very busy day at the Nelson farm. Mom and Dad finished packing for their trip to Russia. The family had a special time of prayer in the morning, after breakfast, to ask God's blessings on their trip and to protect the children while Mom and Dad were gone. As they rose to their feet, Andy could see that Mom had been crying.

"It's okay," Cathy reassured her. "I'm sure that things are going to go well for you in Russia, Mom."

Mom pulled out a Kleenex and wiped her eyes. "I know," she nodded, about to start crying again. "There are just so many things happening. I'm happy for all of it, except for having to leave you children behind."

"We'll be okay," Andy said cheerfully. "Grandad is going to take good care of us while you're gone."

"I know," Mom agreed. "But I won't be with you. I'm going to miss seeing you come down the stairs each morning . . ." Mom stopped talking and turned to Dad, who gave her a hug.

"You know that we almost never leave you children," Dad added. "That's why it's so hard. We're a happy family and enjoy being with each other." Then, seeing that Ben was looking like he was going to cry, Dad offered this diversion: "Say, why don't we call that vet and see if we can find out who the mysterious dog belongs to?" As he walked toward the phone, things seemed to brighten.

"Do you have the phone number?" Dad asked Andy.

"Yes sir!" Andy pulled out his notebook and turned quickly to the clues for the Case of the Unknown Dog. "Here it is." Dad dialed as Andy read off the phone number.

"Can I see your notes?" Dad requested, still holding the phone. "I need the tag number . . . Hello," he answered as the vet's office picked up. "Apparently someone has lost a dog and it came to our house. It has a tag with your phone number on it . . . Yes, there is an ID number . . . It's 0023898 . . . Timothy Nelson . . . my phone number is . . . Okay, thank you very much." Dad hung up the phone.

"Well, whose dog is it?" Jason asked before Dad could even finish hanging up the phone.

"I don't know," Dad replied.

"You mean the Case of the Unknown Dog continues?" Andy asked. He couldn't believe it.

"For a few minutes, anyway," Dad laughed. "They wrote the number down and will have to look it up and call us back. They're very busy now because one of the office staff called in sick today. The lady I talked to was someone from a temporary employment agency. She's really just answering the phones for them. She said they would call back as soon as they could."

"Thanks for trying, Dad. I guess we'll just have to wait," Andy sighed.

Mom got all of the children started in their homeschooling lessons. This morning the older boys were studying about the history and geography of Russia. It was an especially exciting subject since Mom and Dad were heading there.

After some time, Mom said that the children could have a break. Andy and Jason walked outside. "Let's go over our clues and try to figure it out one more time," he suggested to Jason.

Jason pulled out his notebook and read over the clues. "My guess is that someone dropped a dog off just to get rid of it. None of our close neighbors are missing a dog."

"We never did hear from Mr. Cartwright," Andy reminded him. "On the other hand, I don't think he would have gotten a dog. But if someone did just drive by and drop off a dog, wouldn't they have taken the tags off first?"

"I didn't think of that," Jason said. "Of course, that would only make sense."

"Maybe they just forgot to, though," Andy offered. "And it was a bad stormy night. That would be a good night to drop a dog off, since no one could really see you doing it or anything."

"Okay, so it could be that someone dropped the dog off. What other explanation could it be?"

The boys thought. "Maybe it just ran away from its home," Ben suggested. "And its home isn't real close to ours."

"We've thought of that," Jason said. "That's a good idea. It's too bad that we can't ride our bikes all over the place trying to find out."

"We could call families," Andy offered, "just to see if they have lost a dog."

"Yes, we could. On the other hand, we'll know

the owner's name pretty soon. I'd hate to bother people when we'll know soon. Say, we could get a map, though, and try to figure out some roads that it might have come from. Then when we do find out, if it is from someplace nearby, we'll see how far off we are."

Ben joined the pair when they borrowed their dad's plat book with his permission. This book showed all the parcels of land in their county with the names of owners identified. "Look at all the farms and houses!" exclaimed Ben. "I didn't know there were so many people living out here."

"Some of the squares just represent land. There's no house or anything on them," Jason explained.

The boys studied the plat book for some time. It was interesting to learn how the parcels of land fit together and contoured around lakes, rivers, and streams. It really helped the boys understand the layout of the county as well as the layout around their own farm. "This is really helpful," Jason concluded. "We should have studied this before. It could help us on some of our mysteries sometime."

After looking at the plat book for a while, the boys identified five roads that they thought might be where the dog came from, if in fact it just got lost from its home. As they were closing the book, the phone rang. The boys ran to the kitchen in time to see Cathy answering it.

"Hello . . . No, I'm sorry but he can't come to the phone right now . . . Yes, we are the ones that found a dog . . . Oh, you did! Good . . ." Cathy looked around, trying to find a piece of paper and pencil. Andy raced over and handed her his notebook and pen.

"I can hardly wait," Jason whispered to Andy.

". . . Yes, I'm ready . . . Dorothy and Arthur Maxwell . . . Okay . . . 2935 West Spring Creek Road . . . 442-3434 . . . Yes, I have it. Thank you so much! Goodbye." Cathy hung up the phone, and turned around to tell the boys. But the boys were not in the room. All three had run to look at the plat book.

"Look! Spring Creek Road was one of the roads we thought it could be, partner!" Jason exclaimed. The boys were very excited. Running back to the kitchen, they nearly ran over Cathy, who was looking for them.

"Slow down, guys," she said, catching Ben in her arms. "I guess you heard."

"Yes, and that is one of the roads that we had thought it might have come from," Andy said, offering Cathy the plat book to look at. "Do you think we can call them?"

"I think that would be okay," Cathy assented.

Andy went to the phone and dialed the number. As it rang, he looked back at Jason with a happy look on his face. Jason returned the smile, along with a thumbs-up. Andy continued to stand there with the phone in his hand. Soon, he covered the mouthpiece and said quickly, "Jason, it's an answering machine. What should I do?"

Jason thought quickly. "Go ahead and leave a message."

"Hello, this is Andy. We found a dog." Jason whispered something to Andy. "Oh, yes. I need to say that I'm Andy Nelson. We found a dog that the vet said belongs to you. It's a Kerry Blue Terrier.

The Farm Mystery Series

Would you please give us a call? Thank you." Again, Jason whispered to Andy. "And our phone number is . . . Thank you." Andy hung up the phone and looked at the clock. "11:05. I hope they call soon."

Mom came into the kitchen. "Hi, guys. It's about time I started making some lunch. I know you boys are hungry."

"Maybe a little," Andy said.

"A little?" Mom was worried. Here were boys that never seemed to be full. "You aren't sick, are you? And we're taking our trip today!" she exclaimed in alarm.

"No ma'am," Jason laughed. "We're just excited. Mom, the vet called and told us who owned the dog. We called them and left a message on their answering machine. We can't wait for them to call back."

They didn't have to wait long. In a few minutes, the phone rang and Mom answered it, while continuing to work in the kitchen. ". . . Well, that's fine . . . Yes, anytime would be fine . . . Okay, goodbye."

"They'll be here in about ten minutes," Mom said. "Would you boys make sure the dog is ready to go?"

"Did they say what happened? When did they lose the dog? Was it during that bad storm? Why haven't they seen our sign?" The questions addressed to Mom were numerous.

"No, boys, she didn't tell me much. Only that her children had been very sad and couldn't wait to get Sam, that's the dog's name, back again. They are on their way over now."

The boys ran to find the dog. It had remained near the front door almost the entire time. Opening the front door, they discovered that the dog was gone.

Chapter Seven

It's gone!" exclaimed Jason. "Here, dog!" he shouted. "How can it have disappeared when it was here by the door all this time?"

Andy couldn't believe it either. However, they looked all around the house and the outbuildings but couldn't find the dog anywhere. "Great! Now we have this family coming to pick it up, and the children all excited about seeing their dog again and it's gone. What a mystery!"

Mom had heard the boys shouting and came outside. "What's wrong, boys? Where's the dog?"

"We can't find him, Mom," Andy explained with concern. "We've looked everywhere. We even tried calling for him."

Mom looked concerned too. "The lady sounded so excited on the phone. I hope we can find him." The sound of a car could be heard coming down the road. The car slowed as it neared the Nelsons' driveway, and then pulled in. "Here they are."

"What do we do?" asked Jason.

"We'll just have to explain," Mom answered, walking toward the car. Two little children had already jumped out, and the parents were opening their doors.

"Where's Sam?" the little girl asked, with a face that was all smiles.

"Well, now, I'm not sure," Mom began. Then she had an idea. "Why don't you call him?"

"Sam! Sam!" the little girl called.

"Look!" Andy exclaimed, pointing across the road. The tall grass was moving and a small object could be seen bounding through the brush. The little girl continued to call. Soon, the little dog came into view and crossed the road.

Sam ran right up to the little girl. If the Nelsons thought they had seen the dog wagging his tail before, they hadn't seen anything yet. The dog twisted and turned and wagged and jumped all around the children and their parents. The little boy and girl were laughing.

"Thank you, Mrs. Nelson." Mrs. Maxwell had tears in her eyes. "We had about given up all hope. We've looked everywhere."

"You're welcome," Mom returned. "Actually, the boys here have been trying hard to find the owners for several days." Mom described how the dog had shown up on Friday night, and how the boys had tried to locate the owners.

"Thank you, boys." Mr. Maxwell reached into his back pocket and pulled out his wallet. "I'd like to pay you a reward for all your hard work."

"Oh, no sir!" exclaimed Jason. "Thank you, but we don't need any money. We're just glad you found your dog."

"Maybe you could help us, though," asked Andy. "We have a few questions that keep bothering us."

"Sure, what are your questions?"

Andy pulled out his spiral notebook. "The dog, I mean Sam, seemed to act like this was his home.

Midnight Sky

Also, why did he show up during that bad storm we had? Do you have any ideas?"

Mr. Maxwell stroked his beard. He looked at the Nelson house as he began talking. "Actually, I have an idea why he might think this was his home. Our house looks a lot like yours. Oh, it's not exactly like yours, but it is about the same color and has a front stoop that is shaped in a half-circle, just like yours. Also, our house sits low to the ground like yours does. As to why Sam seemed to adopt your family, I'm not sure. He's a very easy-going dog and loves people. He usually stays inside at our house so he can be near us all the time. Other than that I can't be sure.

"Now, why did he show up during the storm? Well, just before dark on Friday night, the children and I were taking him for a walk through our woods. Suddenly Sam sprinted off, like he was on the trail of something. He may have smelled a deer or a racoon or something, I don't know. Anyway, he took off from us. About that time the first peals of thunder and flashes of lightning occurred. I was concerned for the safety of my children and myself, so we headed back toward the house."

"I don't blame you," Andy said.

"It was a bad storm, I could see that," Mr. Maxwell continued. "I called back to Sam, and expected him to follow as he has always done. Then the rain began and I scooped up my children and ran faster toward the house. By then, I wasn't thinking of the dog at all. When we were inside, Alice cried out, 'But where's Sam, Daddy?' Looking out the window I didn't see anything except sheets of rain. I couldn't go looking for him in the storm but promised to do so in the morning. I told her he was probably already in the barn or somewhere out of the rain. He's a pretty smart dog.

"In the morning, I went looking for him all over our woods but couldn't find him. Of course, any tracks that he might have made were washed out by the storm. I sort of thought he might have gone down by the stream, so I walked along it in both directions but couldn't find him."

"That same stream goes right through our property!" Jason exclaimed, remembering the details he had seen in the plat book.

Mr. Maxwell scratched his head. "Yes, that would make sense, then. He probably followed the stream to your farm. On Saturday and Sunday, we didn't drive over this way, because we couldn't believe he would come this far. Of course, that was assuming he had used the roads or open fields. If he followed the stream, it wouldn't be as far. Sure, that makes sense!

"Anyway, I called the newspaper this morning and put an ad in the paper seeking our lost dog. I also put posters up at the grocery store, bank, and hardware store asking for information about Sam. I did offer a reward," he repeated, looking at the boys.

"We really don't need a reward," Andy replied. "Just having you answer our questions is reward enough for us. Thanks!"

The children thanked the Nelsons too, then the Maxwells got back in their car. Sam rode in the back seat between the children.

Andy and Jason waved as the car drove away. "I'm going to miss him," Andy sighed. "I liked that little dog."

"Me too," Jason agreed. "But look on the bright side! The Case of the Unknown Dog is now solved," he said, making an entry in his notebook.

"And," Andy added, "it's lunch time!"

Chapter Eight

After lunch, the boys worked on compositions about Russia until it was time for Grandad to arrive. He lived about forty-five minutes from the Nelsons and had agreed to stay with the children while Mom and Dad were in Russia.

Before long, Mom suggested that the boys stop working on their compositions. "I think that's enough for today," she said, smiling. The boys were having trouble keeping their minds on their school work due to the many things that were coming up. It wasn't every day that Grandad came or that Mom and Dad left for Russia!

Even though it was pretty weather outside, the boys wanted to be inside, probably to be near their parents as much as they could. Since Mom and Dad had been talking about their upcoming flight to Russia, Ben and Andy decided to pretend to fly an airplane. Ben was wearing overalls, a white T-shirt, and had a red bow tie snapped to one side of the overall bibs. He was sitting on the piano bench which had been backed up to the couch. "I'm the ticket-taker and map-holder," Ben announced as Cathy entered the room. "Do you want to take a trip?" Then in a whisper, he added, "Please say 'Yes!'."

"Well yes, I surely would," Cathy announced, to go along with Ben's request.

"Sorry, you have to have a ticket," Ben replied, looking the other way, as though he were checking in other passengers who **did** have a ticket.

Cathy laughed. "Where do I get a ticket?"

"I'll be with you in a minute, ma'am," Ben said, still punching imaginary tickets from imaginary passengers with a hole-punch. After a minute, he turned to Cathy. "I can help you now. Where did you want to fly?"

"How about Nashville?" Cathy suggested.

"Sorry, we don't go there," Ben informed her. "There's the list of places on the screen," he said, pointing to the living room wall.

"Oh, I see. I would like to fly to Atlanta, then," Cathy decided.

Ben sighed loudly. "Okay, but that ticket takes a long time to stamp." He pretended to take a long time typing something on a typewriter and then handed her a scrap of paper. "Just have a seat over there. We'll call you when it's time."

"I hate to be ungrateful, Mr. Ticket-taker, but I have dishes to do," Cathy reminded.

"Atlanta! Now boarding! All rows now boarding for Atlanta! Please don't push and shove! Women and children first, please! Have your tickets ready!"

"Ben, that's too loud!" Mom admonished, entering the room from the kitchen. She smiled at the scene.

"Yes, Mom," Ben answered. "I mean, yes ma'am, we'll try to keep them more quiet. I'm sorry."

"Here's my ticket," Cathy said, handing Ben the scrap of paper.

Ben examined it carefully. "I'm sorry, ma'am,

but this flight doesn't leave until tomorrow."

"See you tomorrow, then." Cathy stood up to leave the room.

"Wait!" Ben said in desperation. "I see that we have a seat open. Yes, we do! Here it is right here!" He pointed to the couch. "Please be seated, we'll be taking off soon."

"Remember my dishes," Cathy warned.

"Okay, Cathy, it won't take long," confided Ben. "All passengers are on board and buckled in, captain!"

Andy was sitting at one end of the couch with his back leaning up against a very large pillow. It was the kind of wedge-shaped pillow that people use when they are sick in bed but want to sit up and read or eat. However, in this circumstance, the pillow just kept falling off the couch, leaving pilot Andy with no seat back.

Andy was dressed for the job, however. He had on his blue sports coat, white shirt, and a red tie. "Okay then, we'll be taking off soon, ladies and gentlemen. Everyone please remain in their seats until I tell them not to anymore." He pretended to be turning some dials and a steering wheel. "Here we go!"

"This is a really smooth flight," Cathy complimented.

"We're not off the ground yet," Andy replied. "We were just taxiing to the runway. Now, here we really go!"

"It's still a smooth flight," Cathy repeated.

"Thank you," Andy returned.

"We have tonpoons!" Ben said confidentially to Cathy.

"Tonpoons?"

"He means pontoons," Andy corrected.

"Yes, and we're going over water right now. We use them every time we go over water."

"What do you use them for?" asked Cathy.

"To land on the water, of course," said the little ticket-taker.

"Splash! Wshoosh! Wshoosh!"

"What's going on?" asked Cathy, smiling, trying to sound concerned.

"We were just going through a car wash for planes," Ben remarked calmly. "There's no need to fear. Captain Andy has many years of flying experience. Right Andy?"

"Actually, this is my first flight," Andy admitted.

"That's okay," Ben said. "He's ten, so he's good." Then in an alarmed tone, he added, "Oh no, our wings just snapped right off!"

"I guess that better be the end of our flight," Andy said. "And look here. Isn't that great? Here we are in Atlanta, just where we wanted to end up." He stood up to greet the deplaning passengers. "Thank you for flying with Nelson Airlines," he said, tipping his hat to Cathy. "We hope you'll choose our airline the next time you fly."

"More than likely I will!" came Cathy's reply. "I'm off to visit relatives in Atlanta, you know."

"Oh?" asked Captain Andy.

"Yes," Cathy responded. "Their names are Mr. Bowls, Mrs. Spoons, and Pastor Forks. I have many other friends to visit. Good day, sir!"

"That was fun!" exclaimed Ben. "But we need

more passengers. Hey Mom . . ." he began, his voice trailing off as he walked into the kitchen.

Before long, Grandad pulled into the driveway. All the children ran out to greet him. Although it had only been a few weeks since they had seen him, the children all loved Grandad. He had Dad's sense of humor and was always ready to read a book or go for a walk with a child.

"Hello, boys!" Grandad greeted them. "Looks like we're going to have some fun for a few weeks. Who knows? Maybe you'll make a farmer out of me yet!" Grandad wasn't raised on a farm and didn't know much about taking care of animals or fixing things up, as was so often the job on a farm.

"Oh, Grandad, you don't need to be a farmer!" exclaimed Ben. "You're a grandad. That's good enough."

"Thanks, Ben," Grandad said. "Where's everyone else?" They all walked into the house.

Soon it was time for Mom and Dad to leave. "Did you get the papers, honey?" Mom reminded Dad, after the luggage was in their car.

"Yes, thanks for reminding me, though. I would hate to fly all the way to Russia and then have to come all the way back home for our paperwork!" Dad said.

After going over one more time the many lists that had been prepared, and checking to make sure everything looked in good shape, Dad asked for everyone to come together by the car for one more prayer. "Dear Heavenly Father, we thank You that you have presented us the opportunity of going to Russia and adding to our earthly family. Please prepare our new children who are in Russia right now for the adoption that is going to take place. We pray they won't be afraid of us and will be happy for new parents. We ask that we will display the love of Christ to them and to everyone else we come in contact with in Russia. Please protect our children while we're gone. Please give Connie and me safety as well, and help us all to be reunited very soon. Your will be done. In Jesus' name, amen." After hugs, tears, and waves, Mom and Dad climbed into the car and soon it disappeared around a bend.

Chapter Nine

Grandad was a wonderful blessing during the next several weeks. He seemed to have a knack for knowing when the children were missing their parents and would arrange something fun and different to do. Once he took them to the zoo, something they all enjoyed doing, but which was more special because they were treated to Grandad's unique comments on the animals. Almost every day, he would take all the children on a long walk through the woods, pointing out signs and identifying plants. Several times they visited the library, and Grandad picked out books that they hadn't remembered reading before. His style of reading made the evenings go by quickly.

Of course, things on the farm had to go on, even though Mom and Dad were away. The children had homeschooling lessons to complete and the animals needed water, food, and attention. Cathy and the boys were able to do all the chores, while Grandad watched. He learned, but said he would let them do the chores. "I might hold the pitchfork wrong or something," he said, laughing.

Once during a thunderstorm, several colts got scared and somehow got out of their corral. It was quite an exciting time for a while until they were back in. Grandad stood behind a fence and called out instructions to the children. He didn't really trust horses, and said so many times. However, all in all, Grandad fit right in and felt comfortable in the Nelsons' house.

"Jason, do you know where your dad keeps his hammer and nails?" Grandad asked one morning, holding a picture in his hand. "I'm afraid I knocked this off by accident and I can't find the nail that was holding it up. I'd like to fix it."

"Sure, Dad has a lot of hammers," Jason answered. "I'll run to his shop and get one." As Jason raced out of the room, Grandad called after him. "And don't forget the nail!"

Jason smiled and said "Yes sir!" Before long he was in his dad's workshop, reaching for the organizer that held an assortment of nails. "Better get two in case Grandad drops one or something," he thought out loud. Choosing a hammer, he turned to go but something caught his eye. For a minute he wasn't sure what had attracted his attention to the west side of the shop. *Must be losing my mind or something*, he thought after scanning that area and seeing nothing out of the ordinary. Then he had another thought. *Maybe a mouse ran along the wall and I just barely saw it.*

At the door he turned to close it behind him. His eyes drifted back to the west side of the shop. *Something's not right*, he thought. Curious, he walked back into the shop and walked to the other side. *But what can it be?* Everything seemed to be in its proper place. Dad was careful to make sure his shop stayed neat and tidy. "If you don't stay organized and uncluttered, how can you ever hope to find anything?" was one of Dad's mottos.

Jason looked at the tools hanging on the wall. What a neat assortment Dad had! There were pipe clamps, T squares, saw blades, c clamps, push sticks, and spring clamps. Also, at this side of the shop Dad had placed his table saw and sander/grinder. Jason could hardly wait until he was old enough to use these power tools all by himself. Yet, Dad was careful and wanted to make sure his boys were old enough not just to use the tools, but also old enough to remember to use the tools safely.

Jason reached over and touched the smooth cast iron surface of the table saw. Maybe this summer, Dad would let him use it some more. As he thought about this, his eyes looked along a shelf that was positioned next to the wall by the saw. "Wait a minute!" Jason exclaimed out loud. "Where's the Sawzall®?" The portion of the shelf devoted to storing this important tool was empty. He dropped down on his hands and knees and searched all around the area. It wasn't there. Quickly, he looked around the shop but it was nowhere to be found. *And that is one of Dad's newest tools*, he told himself. *Boy, he's going to be upset if someone has stolen it!* Yet, what other explanation was there?

Jason ran back to the house, and almost ran into Grandad who was standing near the back door. "Whoa there, young man!" Grandad said, smiling. "You're liable to get a ticket for going 50 MPH in a 5 MPH zone. And I don't see a hammer or nail. Couldn't you find one?"

"I'm sorry, Grandad," Jason panted, totally out of breath. "It wasn't there! I mean the hammer was there. But the other is gone!" In his excitement, Jason was having trouble putting his thoughts into words and they came tumbling out, confusing his grandfather. Andy, who was carrying a load of laundry up from the basement, stopped to listen to Jason.

"Hold on there, helper!" Grandad said. "You're losing me pretty fast. Why don't you start over and go a little slower this time?"

Jason took a deep breath and then began again. "Andy, do you know if Dad took his reciprocating saw anywhere and didn't bring it back to the shop?"

"Yes. I mean, no, he didn't leave it anywhere. Remember how Dad used it just a few days before he and Mom left on their trip? He cut out that panel in the barn with it. But he put it back on its shelf in the shop. I was carrying his extension cords back for him, and saw him put it there." Andy thought another minute. "I'm pretty sure it was there right before Dad left for Russia, because I had to go into the shop and get Dad a tool to fix one of his suitcases. Yes, I know it was there because I looked over at it. That bright shiny red carrying case is neat and I always look at it!"

"Well, it's not there now," Jason announced, importantly.

Grandad joined the conversation. "I'm sure it's probably out there somewhere, boys. We can go out and look for it if you want. Is it an expensive tool?"

"I don't know," Jason said. "But Dad sure is careful with it. It's almost brand new and he hasn't used it much at all."

"It must be pretty expensive," Andy added. "He talked about getting it for quite a while before he finally went to the hardware store and bought it. I know he had been looking at them just about every time we went to the hardware store for a long time." After a minute, he added, "It would be a pretty easy thing for someone to steal!"

By this time, Ben had walked up to the trio and was listening intently. "I know where it is."

"You do?" asked Grandad, relieved. "Well, why don't you show us? These brothers of yours seem a little worried about that tool."

"Okay," Ben said, walking toward the front door.

"It's not in the shop," Jason informed him, following behind his little brother. "I've already looked there."

Ben didn't say anything and kept walking. "He's walking to the shop." Andy was exasperated. "He doesn't know where it is."

Grandad was not so convinced. "Let's give him a chance, boys. Maybe he knows somewhere that your dad put it in the shop."

Ben opened the shop door and walked straight to the shelf on the west side of the shop. He pointed down to the empty place. "Right there."

"I don't see it!" Jason said. "Where is it?"

"It's supposed to be right there on that shelf." Ben seemed pleased with this knowledge that he possessed.

"You're right, it's **supposed** to be there. But it's not," Andy emphasized. "Do you know where it is, then?"

Ben shook his head.

"Why don't we look in here really well?" Grandad suggested, scanning the shop. "There are a lot of tools in here. Let's see if it's in here somewhere." Then picking up an electric circular saw, he asked, "This isn't it, is it?"

"No sir. What we're looking for is kept in a shiny

new red metal case with the word Sawzall written on the top. The case is about this big," he said, holding out his hands to show its approximate size.

"Oh, I see," Grandad nodded. "What do you do with this saw?"

"You use it to cut metal or wood," Jason explained. "Basically it's a blade that goes back and forth without you having to do anything. You mostly use it to cut shapes with. And you can make it cut any depth you want by adjusting a shoe near the blade. Dad uses ours mostly to rough-cut out things. Like if he needs to cut a hole in a wall, he uses his Sawzall to do it. It can cut right through studs, plaster, nails, anything! The blade can go back and forth almost 3,000 times a minute! It's a really neat tool."

"Sounds dangerous, too," Grandad offered.

The team looked everywhere in the shop but couldn't find the tool.

"Shouldn't we call the police?" Andy questioned. "Someone probably stole it while we were all gone somewhere with Grandad."

Grandad thought about it for a minute. "That might be good advice and I might take it," he said. "But I want to give it a little time first. It might show up somewhere else. And hopefully, your dad will call from Russia. If he does, we'll ask him."

"But couldn't the police start looking for it now?" Jason asked.

"You would think so," Grandad answered. "I'm not saying that they wouldn't do everything they could to help find it, because they would. But unless someone left it on the highway or someplace obvious, that would be a mighty hard thing to find. Given the dimensions you gave me, it could be hidden anywhere. Besides, I assume that this tool you're talking about is fairly common. Right? Would you think that lots of people own them?"

Andy nodded.

"In that case it would be difficult to prove that a tool someone was using was your dad's tool. It could be done, certainly, by using serial numbers and things like that. But it would hardly be worth the police department's time to investigate. Am I making sense?"

"I think so," Jason acknowledged. "They need to spend lots of time helping people in accidents, and finding criminals who have committed bigger crimes."

"Exactly," Grandad said. "We'll still call them if we find out for sure that it's been stolen. But let's follow my plan first, okay?"

"Okay," Andy agreed. "Hey, shouldn't we see if anything else is missing?"

"Good idea," Jason responded. Jason and Andy looked carefully around the shop. They looked in drawers and on hooks. Ben also seemed to be trying to look. He looked in the garbage can and under a pile of wood.

"Hey, what about Dad's chop saw?" Andy asked. "It usually just sits up on his bench, but it's not there."

"You're right!" Jason agreed. "I'll run and see if it's in the barn anywhere." He was back in a few minutes. "No, it wasn't there. Well, that makes two tools that are missing!"

Andy had pulled out his notebook and was jotting down notes about the Case of the Missing Tools. "Yes, and those are pretty expensive tools, too."

"What does a chop saw look like?" Grandad asked. "And what do you use one for?"

"A chop saw has a round blade on it that goes around real fast," Ben offered. "And Dad turns it on, puts his wood under it and pulls down on a handle, slamming the saw down into the wood!"

"That's right," Andy said. "It is used to make very clean cuts in wood. The blade can be turned so you can cut very exact angles. Dad uses it a lot when he is installing trim in the house or anytime he needs to cut an exact angle."

"Trim?"

"You know, like baseboards and chair rails. Things like that."

"Of course," Grandad said. "He used that tool at my house one time. Well, does it look like anything else is missing?"

Although the boys looked carefully, they didn't find any other tools missing.

Grandad noticed the concern on the boys' faces. "Don't worry guys, I'm sure they'll turn up. Maybe your dad let someone borrow them. I'll ask him if he calls from Russia, okay?"

As they were walking out, Andy had a good idea. "Let's lock Dad's workshop. He keeps this key hidden over here." Andy slid a piece of wood to the left, exposing a key. "Maybe we can keep other tools from disappearing while we're away."

"That is a good idea," Grandad said. "I don't think a thief would ever be able to find where that key is hidden. That's a pretty neat hiding place."

"Dad made it," Ben announced. "He does lots of neat stuff."

As they were walking toward the house, Grandad suddenly thought of something. "Hey, what about my hammer and nail?"

Jason turned around quickly and returned to the shop. He met the group inside the house and handed Grandad the hammer and nail. "Here you go. Sorry. I guess I was thinking about our tools too much."

"It is something to think about," Grandad agreed.

Chapter Ten

Well, now we have a new mystery to solve, The Case of the Missing Tools, " Jason said later that day in the office of The Great Detective Agency. "And a pretty important one, too."

"Grandad didn't seem too worried about it," Andy suggested. "I don't know why. Maybe it's just because he doesn't know much about tools."

"At least the door is locked now. That should help keep Dad from losing any more tools. What clues do we really have?"

Andy looked at his notebook. "Nothing really. Just that the Sawzall and chop saw are missing, that's all."

"I guess we're going to have to keep a close eye on the shop," Jason suggested. "You know, check on it several times a day to see if anything else turns up missing. Do you have a pretty good idea what all is out there? I think I would spot something if anything was missing, how about you?"

"Yes, I do too," Andy said. "I mean I might not miss a single socket or something like that. But I spend so much time looking at Dad's tools that I know what he's got."

"Good," Jason concluded. "Then, we'll just keep a good eye on the shop and see if any more clues turn up." That seemed to be all the boys could do right now, so the official meeting of The Great Detective

Agency was dismissed.

They kept a good eye on the shop each day. Of course, there were times when Grandad took the children off the farm, but Andy and Jason almost always went straight to the shop upon their return.

On Friday, Grandad took the children to the grocery store after the morning homeschooling lessons were finished. "We need to get some more peanut butter," he said. "Do you guys always eat so much so quickly?"

"I think that maybe they're putting it on a little more thickly than usual since Mom and Dad are gone," Cathy suggested.

"Well, that's okay," Grandad decided. "I don't think it'll hurt them to have a little more peanut butter."

After they returned from the store, Andy and Jason helped unload the groceries they had bought. "We only went for a few things, but look what all we brought home!" exclaimed Andy. "Grandad sure likes to buy things." Finally, all the bags were in the house for Cathy to unload and put away.

"Let's go see if there are any more clues about the Case of the Missing Tools," Jason offered. The boys raced to the shop.

Andy reached to move the piece of wood behind which the key was hidden, but stopped suddenly. "Look," he said, pointing.

The piece of wood had obviously been moved by someone or something. The key was partly visible to anyone walking by.

"Are you sure you closed the wooden piece back all the way?" Jason asked.

Midnight Sky

"Remember that you were the one who closed it last," Andy reminded him. "After I had closed it, you had to go back and get the hammer and nails for Grandad. Did you close it back?"

"That's right! Yes, I closed it well. I even looked at it a second to see if anyone could figure out how to open the wood to get at the key. I was sure it was well camouflaged."

"In that case, we may have had a visitor. What should we do?" asked Andy.

Jason tried the door. It was locked tight. "I guess we need to go in and see if anything is missing. And hopefully see that someone brought back Dad's tools."

Andy took the key and turned the lock. The boys entered the darkened room in silence. Something moved in the north side of the shop. "Just a mouse, sounds like to me, "Andy offered quietly.

Jason switched on the lights and the room seemed more inviting. "The chop saw is still missing," he said, looking at the bench. "So is the Sawzall. Let's see if anything else is gone."

The boys combed the shop for missing tools. They started at the bench area, looking at the wrenches, screwdrivers, and socket sets. Nothing seemed moved. Then they each started examining opposite sides of the room.

"Uh oh," Jason announced. "Dad's air compressor is gone!" Andy quickly moved beside Jason. "I know it was here last time we were looking. I remember it."

Andy pulled out his notebook and took some notes. So did Jason. After a minute, Andy said quietly, "We better see if anything else is gone."

After their search was concluded, they had discovered only one additional missing item: a pneumatic stapler.

"Those are some pretty expensive items," Andy observed. "I wonder if someone is stealing them and then selling them."

"Maybe," Jason somewhat agreed. "But if they wanted to make money, why wouldn't they steal the socket sets and hand tools? Those things are very expensive and yet easy to carry off. But we haven't seen one of them disappear."

"Not yet," Andy noted ominously.

The boys searched for additional clues. All the windows were locked and didn't look like they had been opened. The large front door, which was actually a garage door so that Dad could bring in bigger pieces of equipment to work on, was securely fastened and locked. It was always locked and could only be opened from the inside. It didn't look like it had been disturbed.

"Hey look, Andy! Here's a print in the dust on this shelf. Looks like someone rested their hand here as they picked up the pneumatic stapler."

"Great!" Andy said. "Don't disturb it. The police may be able to use it to find the thief. Then a thought crossed his mind. "It's too bad that we didn't think of that before. I wouldn't be surprised if the key had his finger prints on it, too. Well, it's too late now. Our fingerprints have probably messed up the thief's prints."

"What should we do with this clue?" Jason asked, looking at the print on the shelf.

Midnight Sky

"Why don't we try drawing it?" Andy suggested.

The boys tried drawing the hand print. After a minute the two boys exchanged drawings. Both laughed. "Yours looks kind of like a turkey," Jason said. "Which is better than mine! Mine looks like one of those tiny, tiny animals that live in ponds that Mom was showing us a picture of."

"You mean an amoeba?" Andy asked. When Jason nodded, Andy laughed. "I knew it looked like something I had seen before!"

The boys decided that, given their lack of drawing ability, they should measure the print, which they did very precisely. Jason got a pair of Dad's precise calipers and took exact measurements of every aspect of the print. It took two pages in their small notebooks to record all of the information. "I'd say that was the most measured print in history," laughed Andy.

After searching for more clues and missing tools, the boys left the workshop. Jason carefully locked the door and had Andy check it too. Jason took the key and wiped it clean on his handkerchief. "Removing our fingerprints," he explained to Andy who was looking at him strangely. Then, using the handkerchief as a "glove," the key was carefully hidden behind the wood and closed up securely. "There, if anyone gets in now, we'll surely know it!"

Andy had a thought. "Shouldn't we take the key inside the house? At least that way the thief can't use it to get in again."

Jason thought about that suggestion. "That makes sense to me. Let's go and tell Grandad and see what he thinks."

The boys raced to the house. They found Grandad in the basement, looking at the sump pump. "Grandad, someone got some more of Dad's tools," Andy said, breathlessly.

After explaining what was missing and the clues they had found, Grandad agreed that the key should be brought into the house. As far as calling the police, Grandad still seemed reluctant. "Your dad hasn't called yet. And they'll be home soon, Lord willing. Let's just wait and see what he suggests when he gets home."

The boys respected Grandad's decision. They knew that he was in charge and his word should be obeyed. After all, he was much older and wiser.

Still, it was hard to suppress their desire to have some officials looking into their mystery. "I guess we'll just have to do the best detective work we can until the police are called. They'll be counting on our information to help find the criminals!" Andy suggested. The boys examined all the clues again closely.

Chapter Eleven

Although Andy enjoyed Grandad, he was really beginning to miss Mom and Dad even more. *I wonder what they're doing right now.* He had such a longing to see them again, that he went to his grandfather. "I know Mom and Dad left you a list of where they would be. Do you know what they are supposed to be doing today?"

"That's an excellent question," Grandad said. "I've got it right here. Each day I look at it and pray especially for what they are supposed to be going through that day. Let's see . . . It says here that today they are supposed to be going before a local judge. If everything has gone perfectly smoothly, they are supposed to be having the final court hearing today."

Andy was excited by that news. He ran to get Jason and Ben to tell them of the news. "Guess what? Today could be the day that we are getting a new brother and sister!" Ben looked puzzled and looked toward the door. "I mean, in Russia. Today is the day that Mom and Dad are having a hearing in front of a Russian judge. Grandad said that meant that the adoption is taking place."

"**If** things have gone smoothly," Grandad reminded. "There is so much red tape that we can't be sure exactly what's going on. However, that's what they hoped to be doing today."

"I know what we should do," Ben said soberly.

"Let's pray."

"That's a very good idea," Grandad agreed. Everyone knelt down there in the kitchen and Grandad led them in prayer. "Dear God, Maker of heaven and earth, we praise Your Name. You alone are worthy of our honor and adoration. We pray for Timothy and Connie right now, both of whom You see and are guiding. May their day go well, within Your holy will. May the adoption be finalized soon so that they can return home and be reunited in safety to their family here. Regardless of what is happening there, we pray that You would help them be a light to that world of Christ's love. May only Your will be done. Amen." The children also prayed.

Andy felt better after praying. Somehow he didn't seem so alone. He knew that God was with him and was also with his mom and dad. The day seemed brighter and Andy even found himself whistling.

During lunch, Grandad tried to cheer everyone up by telling stories about his childhood. Since Grandad had a sense of humor much like Dad, these stories were always much appreciated and enjoyed. "Did I ever tell you about the trip I took to Nashville one time in ol' Blue?"

"No, will you tell us about it?" enthused Andy. "Your stories are always so exciting."

"Well, I'm not sure it will be exciting but I'll tell it to you. When I was eighteen, I bought my first car. It wasn't much of a car, but it was mine. The previous owner had named it ol' Blue. I tried to tell myself that it was named that because it would go as fast as a blue streak, but I'm afraid it was probably a better descrip-

Midnight Sky

tion of the smoke that came out of the tailpipe. After overhauling the brakes, repairing the transmission, and having it painted, I learned that owning a car was an expensive proposition. I remember paying the man $1.50 for Tennessee license tags, which was a lot of money back then, and thought I would never be able to afford to keep a car after all! Well, anyway, I decided to take a trip to see my uncle in Nashville. My friend and neighbor, Jerry Beetle, who everyone called 'Beet,' decided that he would like to drive over with me. That way we could share the expenses and the driving. About halfway to Nashville, with Beet driving, we were passed by an older couple in a new Oldsmobile. They waved politely as they passed. We waved back.

"A moment or two later, I noticed that our car was picking up speed. I looked over at Beet, but his eyes were fixed ahead, staring at the Oldsmobile that had just passed us. Soon Beet was passing the Oldsmobile as though it had completely run out of gas. We were absolutely flying! I waved as I passed the older couple, but they weren't smiling.

"'Beet, don't you think you are going a little too fast?' I asked. At first Beet didn't say anything. He just kept staring at the speedometer. Instead of slowing down, we were still accelerating! 'Beet! Slow this car down!' I shouted to him.

"'Can't,' was his only reply. 'What do you mean you can't?' I asked in exasperation.

"'Car's gone berserk!' Beet informed me. 'It's speeding up all by itself! What do I do? What should I do?!'

"We were traveling at a rate of speed that one

wouldn't think possible of ol' Blue. The tires were drumming, the steering wheel shook and I just knew we were going to crash and be killed." Grandad stopped and spread more jam on his piece of bread. Then he took a bite and smiled at the children.

"Well, what happened, Grandad?" Ben asked.

"You want to hear more?" Grandad smiled. "I guess I could tell you the rest. Let's see now, we were about to crash, weren't we? 'Maybe the accelerator's stuck,' I yelled at the top of my lungs. The noise of the engine was almost deafening. Beet kicked at it to dislodge it, but that didn't do any good. We continued flying down the highway. We were going so fast that we thought it would be disastrous to try to brake or even turn.

"'Do something!' Beet yelled. 'Do something or we're going to die!'

"Finally it came to me. God must have told me what to do. I reached over and turned the ignition key to the off position. We were going so fast that it still took us some time before we were able to feel ourselves slowing down much. Eventually, we were able to pull off the highway. That older couple in the Oldsmobile drove by, moving carefully over into the left lane a little just as they passed by. There were no friendly waves this time."

"What was wrong with the car?" Jason asked.

"Good question," Grandad praised. "As you know, I've never been very mechanically-minded. But here's what Beet did. First, he checked the accelerator linkage. No problem with it. We started the engine again, in neutral of course, but it raced at full throttle and sounded like it was going to explode. We shut off the engine and Beet suggested looking at the carburetor. He took off the air cleaner and could see that a flat piece of metal, I think he called it the throttle plate, had dropped off and was lying loose at the bottom! Such a thing should never be able to happen, but it did to us. Apparently the tiny rivets that held the throttle plate to the rod had somehow loosened over the years. He reattached it with some wire he found in the trunk, temporarily of course, until we could have a mechanic really fix it. But I'll never forget the feeling of riding in a car that was totally out of control."

"Was it hard to get it fixed?" Andy asked.

"Well, that's an interesting story in itself," Grandad said. "We took it to a car repair shop and the owner said that he needed to drill a small hole in order to reattach the throttle plate. He didn't want to risk it."

"Why not? Was he afraid that by drilling he would cause a spark and ignite some gas fumes or something?" Jason wondered.

"No, that wasn't his concern. You see it was wartime and there were always shortages. At that particular time it was hard to secure drill bits. If he broke a drill bit while repairing an old car, it wouldn't be easy to replace."

"You mean he couldn't just go to the hardware store and get another one?" Ben asked in disbelief. "Our hardware store has tons of them."

"I know they do now," Grandad agreed. "But during the war, the store shelves were not stocked as well as they are now. No, things were different back then. It was hard to get all kinds of things, like machinery and machinery parts. They stopped making cars during the war and didn't start again until six months after the war ended. The government even had to ration items like gasoline, rubber, shoes, butter, meats, and sugar. Even with ration coupons these items were sometimes hard to find. Well anyway, the mechanic finally agreed to take the big risk and didn't break his drill bit. So we were back in business again."

"That was a neat story," Ben said. "I like to hear about your life and how things used to be so different than today."

Grandad smiled. He had achieved his purpose. The children seemed in better spirits.

After lunch, the boys weren't sure how to spend their time. They considered riding their bikes, going fishing with Grandad, or pitching some horseshoes. They finally decided on bike riding.

"First, let's see if any more tools are missing," Jason suggested.

In the shop, nothing seemed to be moved and nothing new was missing. After riding their bikes a while the boys returned to the house.

"I wish there was something we could do about the Case of the Missing Tools," Andy said. "Hey, I wonder if we called some of Dad's friends if they would know anything about it?"

"That's a good idea," Jason agreed. He started toward the phone, but stopped. "We better ask Grandad first. He may not want us to call them." But Grandad thought it was a wonderful idea, so Jason made the first call to Mr. Claymore.

"Hello, Mr. Claymore, this is Jason . . . Yes sir,

we're okay . . . No sir, they're still in Russia . . . No, we haven't heard from them . . . Well, yes, I did have a reason for calling. I know that you borrow some of Dad's tools sometimes. Dad says that he is happy that others can use his tools. Anyway, did you happen to borrow his Sawzall recently? . . . Yes, he bought one a few months ago . . . It sure is a nice tool, but . . . No sir, he doesn't let me use it yet . . . I know it's dangerous . . . Well, you see I can't use it while he's gone, even though I never would, because it's missing . . . Yes sir . . . I don't suppose you borrowed his chop saw, air compressor or pneumatic stapler either? . . . I didn't think so, but I'm just checking . . . No, we don't need anything . . . Yes, Grandad is taking care of us . . . Yes, I'll tell Dad to call when he gets back from Russia . . . You have a nice day, too . . . Good bye."

"He hasn't borrowed them," Jason informed Andy with a grin. "But he sure wanted to make sure I wasn't using Dad's power tools while Dad is gone. He kept saying 'I know you wouldn't, but now, don't you go and use them! They can be dangerous you know!'"

"Should we call someone else?" Andy asked.

"Let's try Mr. Kyle and Mr. Mercer," Jason suggested.

Those calls did not result in any more information that would help solve the Case of the Missing Tools. Mr. Kyle did say that he was planning on borrowing the air compressor, but hadn't even talked to Dad about it yet.

"One interesting thing," Jason said, "is that all three men said they always ask Dad before borrowing his tools. I just can't picture one of his friends coming in and getting tools without asking permission."

"Me either," Andy agreed. "Well, when Dad gets home, we'll have to see if he has given anyone permission to borrow them. Seems like he would have told one of us about it, though, so we wouldn't be worried while he was gone."

"Maybe," Jason said. "On the other hand, they were pretty stressed right before they left. There were a million little things they had to do before leaving for Russia, and maybe he just forgot to tell us. I wouldn't blame him if he did."

"Me either. What do we do now?"

"I guess nothing. We will just have to keep checking to see if anything has been moved or taken," Jason suggested.

That night at the table the boys talked about the Case of the Missing Tools. Grandad didn't have any suggestions. He continued to think that someone must have borrowed them and wanted Timothy to handle it himself. The last thing Grandad wanted to do was to accuse someone of stealing tools when in fact they had just been borrowed. He tried to change the subject.

Picking up a strawberry from his plate, he held it in the air. "Take a look at that boys, and Cathy, you look at it too," he said, smiling. "Know what that is?"

The older ones hesitated, not sure what Grandad meant. Ben, however, took the question at face value and answered quickly, "That's a strawberry, Grandad!"

"That's right," Grandad replied. "And do you have any idea how a strawberry tastes?"

The older ones looked at each other. What was

Grandad driving at?

"It tastes like . . . well, it tastes kind of like strawberry jam," offered Ben.

Grandad laughed. "I can't argue with that," he said. "Do the rest of you know what it tastes like?"

They all nodded. Andy was hoping that he would do something neat, like dip it into chocolate or something. He didn't.

"Wouldn't it have been neat to have been Adam, the first man? I mean, think about it. Here he is walking along, and he sees this strawberry plant on the ground. He's never had a strawberry in his life. He reaches down and picks one up. What do you think he would do next?"

"I think he would smell it," Andy responded.

"That's because you are always smelling your food, Andy," Cathy laughed.

"I know," Andy smiled. "But I like to get pleasure from food as many ways as I can. If I didn't smell it, I would only get to enjoy it by tasting it."

"What else might he do?" Grandad probed.

"I think he would hold it in his fingers and see what it felt like. Then I think he would pop it into his mouth!" Jason suggested, laughing.

"I think he would take a bite of it, too," Grandad agreed. "Then he would know what it tasted like. He could decide if it tasted sweet, like a peach, or sour, like a grapefruit. Or hot tasting, like an onion. The point is, that until he ate one, he wouldn't really have any idea how it tasted. Wouldn't that be exciting?"

The children thought that was an interesting thing to think about. Grandad continued. "Suppose he was walking along and saw a cherry?"

"He might think it looked something like a strawberry," offered Cathy. "He would really be surprised, wouldn't he?"

Grandad laughed. "Yes, I can picture him now, taking a good healthy bite into the cherry and hitting the pit. 'Ouch! There's a stone in there!' he might think."

The children thought of other fruits and vegetables and the reaction that Adam might have as he ate them for the first time. Andy was just sure that Adam wouldn't be able to stop eating blueberries when he tried just one, while Jason was equally convinced that Adam wouldn't even be able to finish eating his first piece of eggplant. "I still can't see how anyone can eat eggplant," Jason said, trying to avoid making a face as he said it.

"Yeah, and what if he picked up a pickle?" Ben suggested. "'Whew, that's sour!' he would say."

Everyone laughed. Ben seemed a little defensive. "I think they're sour, anyway."

"Remember that pickles don't just grow out of the ground," Grandad said kindly. "We make them by taking cucumbers and then adding pickling spices to them."

"Oh yeah, I forgot," Ben said, laughing with everyone else.

And so the day went by, like most of them, with Grandad helping the time to not seem so long.

The boys continued to search for clues to the Case of the Missing Tools, but nothing new happened. No new tools were missing and none of the missing tools were returned. "I hope Dad and Mom will be home soon," Jason said, as the boys prepared for bed.

Midnight Sky

"I would like to see if Dad loaned his tools to anyone."

"Me too," Andy agreed. "Grandad said they might be home as early as day after tomorrow. They are going to call when they get back into the United States."

The boys were quiet as they each thought about the return of their parents. It would be so good to see them again. The farm just didn't seem like the same place without Mom and Dad around. *I want to see Dad breaking the colts some more*, thought Andy. *And I wonder what Mom will make for the first meal when she gets home.* With those thoughts, Andy eventually closed his eyes and went to sleep.

Chapter Twelve

The phone was ringing. *I wonder why no one is answering the phone,* thought Andy as he slowly got out of bed and walked downstairs toward the kitchen. Just as he reached the kitchen, however, the back door opened and Grandad came in and quickly walked to the phone. "Hello," he said. Then his face broke into a great big smile. "Timothy! Oh, it's so good to hear your voice, son. Are you back in the States? . . . Great! Did everything go okay? . . . Wonderful! . . . Yes . . . Yes, everything is going great here . . . Most are still in bed, but Andy's right here . . . Sure, you can talk to him." Grandad handed the phone to Andy. "It's your dad!"

Andy could hardly talk, he was so excited. "Hi, Dad . . . Yes sir, we've been good . . . It's good to hear your voice again, too . . . Oh, hi, Mom . . . I love you, too! . . . You will? . . . Great! Yes, I'll tell everyone else . . . Okay . . . Okay . . . Goodbye."

"They just got back to Atlanta, Grandad, and they are going to start home right away! How long will it take for them to get home?"

Grandad looked at the clock. "Well, I would say they might be here by 1:00. Maybe 2:00. It all depends on the traffic and things like that. It sure was good to hear their voices again, wasn't it?"

Andy had tears in his eyes. He was so happy he couldn't stand it. He said, "Yes sir!" then ran out of the kitchen toward his bedroom.

"They're coming home!" Andy shouted as he got to his room. "Wake up, Ben and Jason! Mom and Dad are in the Atlanta airport and they're coming home today!"

Cathy had heard the commotion and soon all the children were in one room laughing and talking. Ben kept throwing his pillow up toward the ceiling and shouting "Yahoo! Yahoo!" over and over.

"Did everything go okay with the adoption?" asked Cathy with a little concern in her voice.

"Yes," Andy said, smiling. "Dad says that I have a new brother and a new sister!"

"Do I?" asked Ben.

Everyone laughed. "Yes," Cathy replied gently. "You have a brother and sister also."

The morning seemed to drag by and Jason and Andy had an especially difficult time concentrating on their math. "If I just had a nickel for every time you children have looked at that clock this morning," Grandad said at lunch, "I think I'd be a rich man. Of course, I've looked at it myself a couple of hundred times. Aren't you boys going to eat your sandwiches?"

"I'm not hungry," Jason admitted.

"Me either," Andy added. "Maybe we will be able to eat after Mom and Dad get home."

"Well, we don't know when that will be. I would hate for you to . . ." Grandad stopped talking because the room was suddenly empty. Grandad jumped up and followed the children to the back door.

Dad's car was pulling into the driveway and the children were jumping up and down and waving at it. Mom and Dad waved back.

"Shhh," Mom whispered as she quickly opened the car door and ran to give everyone a big hug. "Baby Leah is asleep and she has had such a hard time. We need to let her sleep."

Dad greeted his family, then began unbuckling a car seat in the back. A cute little boy climbed out and looked at the boys. "Boys, I'd like you to meet your new brother, Matthew! Matthew, this is Andy, Ben, and Jason. And that's Cathy."

"Hi!" Ben said. "You're my new brother!"

Three-year-old Matthew seemed very shy and slid behind Dad. He then peeked around Dad's leg to look at the children before returning to safety behind Dad. Dad smiled and winked at Ben. "He's just a little shy. He's going to have to learn that you boys are fun to play with and that you love him. We won't rush him. And remember, he doesn't understand much English."

Mom and Dad were happy to see everyone but seemed very tired. In fact, even Dad took a nap; something the boys didn't remember having happened much before. When they got up from their naps, they told Grandad and the children about their trip. Things had gone smoothly in the adoption process.

"Matthew seems to already be responding well to some medicine for his health condition," Dad commented. "It was medicine that the orphanage just couldn't afford. We're thankful that God has allowed us to get it for him."

Leah, however, was quite anemic, and seemed to have very little energy. "She needs lots of good food, sunshine, and love," Mom said, rocking the toddler gently. "She may also need to see the doctor soon. We'll just have to see."

Midnight Sky

After supper, Grandad packed his suitcase and prepared to leave. "Thanks for taking such good care of us," Andy said, hugging his grandfather. "You helped us to have fun even though Mom and Dad were gone. I'm really going to miss you."

"I'll miss you too," Grandad echoed. "I'm going to miss all of you. It's been a long time since I took care of children and I found that I've missed it. But I'll see you all again soon, don't worry about that. I've got to come back and learn more about my new granddaughter and grandson too, you know!" Everyone waved as Grandad drove down the lane.

The next morning, Dad walked out to the barn to check on his animals. "It sure is nice to be home again," he told the boys who were following closely beside him. "I've missed you children terribly. And I've missed my animals, too."

"We missed you, Dad," Ben responded quickly. "It was fun to be with Grandad, but no one is like you. You take big steps!"

Dad smiled and reached over and stroked Ben's hair. "And no one's like you, Ben!"

Dad was pleased with the health and condition of the animals. He began whistling a hymn. As he was forking some hay into one horse stall, Jason began, "Dad, have you let anyone borrow your tools?"

"You know I always let people borrow my tools," Dad replied, not stopping his work. "Why?"

"Well, while you were gone, we found several tools missing. We wondered if maybe you had just let someone borrow them and they hadn't brought them back yet."

The Farm Mystery Series

Dad took out his handkerchief and blew his nose. "Not used to breathing hay dust," he laughed. "Well, I'll get used to it again soon." Then addressing the subject that Jason had raised, he continued. "I don't know. What tools are you talking about?"

Andy pulled out his notebook. "How about your Sawzall, your chop saw, your air compressor, and your pneumatic stapler?"

"That's a pretty big list!" Dad exclaimed, stopping his work. "Read it to me again." As the list was read, Dad was thinking. When Andy was finished, Dad shook his head. "I don't remember anyone asking to borrow those tools. You're sure they're gone?"

"Oh, yes sir! We're sure!" Jason answered. "First, the saws went missing. Then a few days later the air compressor and pneumatic stapler were gone."

Dad removed his hat and rubbed his forehead with his handkerchief. He looked up at the ceiling as if deep in thought. "Now that is a mystery," he finally said. "No, I don't remember anyone asking to borrow those. We'll have to take a look when I'm through here." Dad went back to work but it was obvious he was still deep in thought.

When he was finished with the barn work he wanted to do, he headed toward the shop. Walking quickly up to the door, he almost broke his nose when the door didn't open as he had expected it to do. With all of his forward momentum, his body crashed loudly into the door. "Ouch!" he exclaimed, stepping back and rubbing his nose and his left arm. He tried the door again, but this time more gingerly. "Why won't this door open?"

"We locked it, Dad," Andy said sheepishly, afraid

he was about to get into trouble. Dad's nose was very red and he kept rubbing his shoulder and arm.

"What?" Then remembering what the boys had said about the tools, he continued. "Oh, I guess you wanted to stop someone from getting in. That makes sense." He looked at his nose in the reflection of the glass in the door, and touched it gently. "That really does hurt!" Then he reached over where the key was hidden and moved the piece of wood. The key was gone.

Dad had a concerned look on his face. Jason quickly reassured him. "We took it inside the house, Dad. After we locked the door, someone came back and apparently found the key. So Grandad said it was a good idea to take the key into the house. I'll run and get it."

Jason returned with the key. "I'm sorry about your nose, Dad."

"It's my fault," Dad confessed, trying to smile, but not having much success. "I was in too much of a hurry. It's like I'm always telling you guys. Haste makes waste! Well in this case it should be 'Haste makes pain!'" He tried to laugh, but again, didn't have much success.

When they entered the shop, Ben rushed over to where the Sawzall should be. "See, Dad, it's gone! I knew it was gone, too."

Dad looked over the shop and took some mental notes. "You're right, boys. It looks like those four things are the only things missing. And you don't know anything else about it?"

"Sure we do, Dad," Andy said, pulling out his notebook. He read off the dates, and times that the tools were found missing. He showed Dad the print on the shelf and then read off some of the print's exact dimensions.

After sharing with Dad all of the facts they had, Andy summarized, "And we wanted to call the police but Grandad said we shouldn't. He said that we should wait until you got home and ask you. What are you going to do, Dad?"

Dad thought for a moment. "I think I'll make a few calls to friends and see if anyone has borrowed these tools. That's the most likely explanation I can think of."

"We thought of that too, Dad," Jason said. "We called Mr. Kyle, and Mr. Mercer, and Mr. Claymore. None of them borrowed your tools."

"Well, you boys are very thorough!" Dad commended. "Those are the three men I was going to call first. Humph!" Dad stood staring at the wall, with his hand on his chin. "I'll have to give it some more thought, that's all. Thanks for your detective work, though. I'll keep you up-to-date about what I decide to do."

"Should we keep the shop locked?" Jason asked.

Dad touched his tender nose again. "Son, that might keep any thieves out. But I'm afraid it might also send me to the hospital if I forget again that it's locked and run into it! I'm willing to risk losing more tools in order to save my face." Everyone laughed.

As they moved back toward the house Jason and Andy talked about the Case of the Missing Tools. They were happy that they had helped Dad. "I just wish we could solve it for him," Andy reflected. "Then he wouldn't have to even think about it. The

Midnight Sky

Great Detective Agency will have to think of new things to help solve the mystery!"

Chapter Thirteen

As they entered the house, Mom announced that she was taking Leah to the doctor. "I would just feel better if Dr. Newberry could look her over and see what he thinks. I should be home after lunch. You guys help Cathy take care of the dishes because she has a lot of other work that needs to be done as well."

"Hey, I just realized something. Isn't Dad going to work today?" Andy asked.

"No, he's going to stay home. The mill has given him the rest of this week off to try and get things in order."

As Mom was getting everything ready to go to the doctor, Dad took care of some paperwork in his study. Matthew stayed right by his side. The boys and Cathy worked on homeschooling. Cathy helped the boys with some grammar rules and gave them each a spelling test.

Later that morning, Dad called Jason and Andy to him. "Boys, I'm going to call the police now about the missing tools. You can stop working on your homeschooling for a while, but I want you to stay close to the house so you can answer any questions the police might ask, okay?"

"Yes sir!" both boys said quickly. "We'll be in our office."

The boys moved quickly to their office under the stairs. "Wow, the police are coming! This is getting very interesting." Then trying to act a little more grown up, Andy continued, "What do you think we should do, partner?"

"I think we should make a copy of our clues that we can hand to the police officers when they're here. We can answer their questions, but it may save them some time to have our written observations as well. You know, 'for the files.'"

"Right!" Andy agreed. The boys began the process of comparing notes and writing a very clear copy for the police officers. Jason did it because his handwriting was a little better than Andy's. Then they went outside and paced back and forth in the driveway waiting for the police to show up.

About thirty minutes later, Dad stuck his head out the door and called to the boys. "You don't have to wait on them. You're free to play. There's no telling when the police officers might show up."

"That's okay, Dad," Andy said. "We don't have anything else we'd rather do."

In about thirty minutes a squad car drove slowly in front of the house and then pulled into the Nelsons' driveway. The boys were disappointed. "No sirens or flashing lights or anything," Andy noted, sadly. "And just one policeman."

The police officer sat in his car for a minute talking on his police radio. Then he stepped out of the car and put his hat on. "Hello boys, is your dad at home?" he asked kindly.

"Yes sir, I'll go and get him," Jason volunteered. But Dad was already walking out of the house.

"Hello," Dad greeted.

"You must be Mr. Nelson," the officer said. "I'm

Phil Stiles." The two shook hands. "So, you've had an uninvited visitor to your shop?" he questioned, looking at his notebook. "Why don't you tell me what you know? Is that the shop?" He pointed to a building near the house.

"Yes, it is," Dad answered. The group walked toward the shop, Dad carrying Matthew, while Dad filled Mr. Stiles in on the missing items. "Actually, my boys here were the ones that discovered the missing items. Maybe they can be of more help than me."

Mr. Stiles looked at the boys. He didn't expect much help from them, but decided to humor Dad. "What do you guys know?"

Jason spoke for The Great Detective Agency. "Here is a list of the things that are missing. I got the serial numbers from the warranty information that Dad keeps in his drawer. And here is a list of the dates and times that we found them missing." He handed several sheets of paper to the officer. "Finally, here is a summary of the clues we have."

Mr. Stiles studied the papers carefully. Then he took off his hat, and put it back on. "Good work, men!" he said approvingly. "Good work! Maybe you can show me where this print is that you talk about in your report."

"Yes sir!" Andy and Jason were very excited.

Mr. Stiles listened carefully to what they said and examined the print. Looking at the sheets of paper from the boys again, he asked, "I suppose you boys are The Great Detective Agency?"

"Yes sir," Jason answered. "We don't really have a big business or anything. But we have fun solving mysteries."

Midnight Sky

"You've been helpful," he said, addressing the boys. "I must admit that I wasn't expecting much, but I was wrong. You've done a good job." Then turning to Dad, he added, "As you can imagine, the chances of finding these tools are slim. The thief more than likely sold them right away. Usually to some home-owner who can't believe what a good deal he's getting. Or the thief might just use them himself. Anyway, we rarely can solve a crime like this one. Still, we'll report it to the local pawn shops and keep our eyes open when we arrest someone or investigate another robbery. There is that one-chance-in-a-million that we'll recover the tools. If we do, we'll let you know."

Mr. Stiles wrote a few more facts in his notebook and then asked Dad to sign a form. "Thanks again for your help, boys," Mr. Stiles said as he was about to get into his car. The boys were busy looking at the squad car.

"Say, would you guys like to get in and see my car?"

The boys jumped at the chance. "See that button there? Push it." Andy did and the siren started blaring. Ben came running out of the house. So did Cathy. When Cathy saw that it was just the boys playing with the siren, she shook her head and walked back in. But Ben jumped in the car with the boys when Mr. Stiles offered to let him. Matthew, how-ever, had no interest in getting into a police car.

After turning on the siren and flashing lights, the boys spoke through the PA system that was installed in the car. All this time, the car's police radio was on and the boys were able to hear the conversations between police officers and headquarters. Soon Jason said, "We better let you go now, Mr. Stiles. I know you've got some important things to do. Thanks for letting us see your car!" Andy and Ben also thanked Mr. Stiles and the boys got out of the car.

As he drove away, Mr. Stiles waved to the boys. "He sure was a nice man!" Ben exclaimed.

"Yes, he was," Andy agreed. "But I just hope he can help solve the Case of the Missing Tools."

"Me too," Jason agreed. "Me too."

Chapter Fourteen

Later that afternoon, the boys were searching for something to do. It had been an exciting morning. "Why don't you guys go for a walk in the woods?" Dad suggested. "Matthew is finally warming up a little to Ben. I think he might be willing to play more with Ben if it was just the two of them for a while."

"Sounds like a good idea to me," Jason said. Andy agreed, and the two headed down the path in their woods.

"I wonder what the police are doing right now to help solve our mystery?" Jason asked as they walked.

"Well, if Grandad is right, there probably isn't much they can do," Andy reminded him. "Maybe they're contacting the pawn shops, like Officer Stiles suggested, and maybe they have some system that they can let other police departments know about it."

"I guess you're right," Jason agreed. "There must be some way that police departments talk to each other and share information." He walked a little further. "That would be a neat job. To be able to talk to other departments and tell them what you know. You know what would be even neater? To have a job where all you do all day is collect information from lots of different police departments and use all of that information to solve a crime. That would be fun."

"It sure would." Andy sat on the ground and leaned up against a tree. "It sure is a nice day today!

Hey, I wonder when Dad will make homemade ice cream! It's pretty warm, don't you think? Maybe he'll make some today."

"I doubt it," Jason laughed, as he struggled to break a stick he had picked up. "Sure, it's warmer than it has been, Andy. But . . ." Jason interrupted himself as he struggled to break the stick in his hand. His face turned red and he even grunted. " . . . Dad always waits until it is really summer and hot before he makes ice cream. Besides, I think he's got too much on his mind with Matthew and Leah today." Jason finally broke the stick. What was a supreme challenge just seconds ago, now held no interest, and Jason flippantly tossed the two halves into the trees.

"I would think it would help them relax some," Andy offered hopefully. "Might even make Matthew start talking or something."

The boys sat, enjoying the beautiful day and trying to think of something fun to do.

As though startled by something, Jason cocked his head to one side. "What was that?" he asked Andy, whispering.

Andy didn't reply. He had thought Jason was just talking to himself.

"Hey, Andy, did you hear that noise?" Jason repeated, a little more loudly this time.

Andy instinctively looked at his brother to try to determine the direction in which Jason was listening. Both boys were quiet for a few minutes.

"What sound . . . ?" Andy began to say, but Jason motioned for him to please be quiet. Apparently the sound was happening as Andy was talking.

"Listen . . . there, did you hear that?"

Midnight Sky

"I heard something, but it just sounded like a small limb falling," Andy replied. "There's a little breeze. Maybe the wind just blew a branch to the ground."

Jason shook his head. "No, it wasn't just a limb falling. You must have just heard the end of the sound."

"Well, what did it sound like?" Andy asked quickly. Excitement is contagious and Andy was definitely catching Jason's.

"Tell you in a minute. First let's see if it happens again."

The boys had forgotten about trying to find something to do, and sat very still. They were doing what they loved best. Trying to learn about something they didn't fully understand.

Several minutes had gone by. Andy's leg was cramped from sitting in one position and he desperately wanted to move and shift his weight a little. He was just about to do so, when the sound came again.

"Bump . . . bump. . bump . bump, bump."

Andy, looking at Jason without speaking, merely shrugged his shoulders. "Beats me!"

"That's the third time I've heard it," Jason said. "Every time it does the same thing."

"It sort of sounds like someone dropping something. And then it bounces a few times until it comes to a rest," Andy reflected.

"Yes, it kind of does," Jason agreed. "The time between bumps gets shorter and shorter. It sort of sounds like . . ." But Jason didn't get to finish his sentence because the sound began again.

"Whatever it is, it sure seems like it's going to do

it again and again. Should we go and try to find it?" Andy asked.

"Yes, let's see if we can see what it is," Jason replied. "I think it came from over there," he said, pointing to the west.

"Really? I'm pretty sure I heard it come from that direction," Andy disagreed, pointing to the southeast.

"Maybe we better wait and listen for it again before moving out," Jason suggested. Both boys sat still again.

It was about five minutes before the sound came again. Now, Jason was sure that it was coming from the northwest, while Andy continued to think it was coming from the southeast. "What do we do now?" Andy asked.

Jason didn't know what they should do. Finally, Andy suggested they let a coin toss make the decision for them. They tossed a coin and then moved off in the direction that Andy had pointed. They stopped from time to time, listening for further evidence of the sound's direction, but it didn't happen again. After a while, Andy said, "Maybe I was wrong, Jason. We've not heard it for a while now. Sorry. Maybe you were right and it came from over there. Let's go that way."

The boys changed direction and moved through the woods. After walking for a while, Jason shrugged his shoulders. "I don't think it's going to happen again. Why don't we take a few notes and then try to solve the mystery?"

"Sure! That's a great idea," Andy agreed. He pulled out his small notebook and wrote at the top of a new paper 'The Case of the Strange Bump.' Seeing that title on paper got him tickled and both boys began laughing.

"We sure do have some strange mysteries to solve," Jason said, looking at his watch to record the exact time of day in his notebook. "But I never thought the time would come when we tried to solve a mystery about a bumping sound." Even though it sounded funny, both boys took careful and serious notes.

After listening quietly for a few more minutes, the boys decided to continue their walk through the woods.

"What do you think it is?" Andy asked. The thought had been on both boys' minds.

"I really don't know," Jason replied. "I need to hear it some more. Right now, the thing that keeps coming to my mind is a bowling ball."

"A what? Did you say a bowling ball?" Andy couldn't believe he had heard Jason correctly.

"Don't laugh," Jason said, smiling. "I didn't say I thought that was what it was. It's just that is what it sounded like to me, for some reason. Think of this. You're at a bowling alley and you pick up your bowling ball above your head. Now drop it. What would that sound like?"

"It would sound like me screaming," Andy answered.

"Why would you scream?" Jason asked, confused.

"Because the bowling ball just landed on my head!" Andy laughed.

"I didn't say you were supposed to drop it on your head," Jason returned.

"Well, the scene you just described had me hold a ball over my head and drop it. Where was the ball supposed to go, Jason?"

"On the bowling alley lane. You know, on the wooden floor that bowling alleys have."

"Okay. Now I've got it. I'm glad it didn't fall on my head, even in a story." Andy laughed again. "And so you think it sounds like that bowling ball dropping to the floor and then bouncing up and down until it finally stopped bouncing?"

"Exactly," Jason replied, tossing a rock into the air. He was trying to throw it over the top of a tree, but wasn't successful. Instead, a small bird came flying fast out of the tree.

Andy just couldn't think seriously. He began to laugh again. Jason looked at him, a little offended that Andy would laugh at his suggestion. "I'm sorry, Jason. I'm not laughing at you. I was just thinking about what you said and then I had this picture in my mind of us going around a curve in our path in the woods, and there is this bowling alley all set up and people bowling. Funny that we never stumbled on that bowling alley before!"

"That would be funny," Jason agreed. "But you do understand that I don't really think it's a bowling ball that's making the sound. It just sounds like one."

"I understand," Andy nodded. "Actually, that's a pretty good description of what it sounds like. Now, since we know, or at least are pretty sure, that there isn't a bowling alley around here in the woods, what could it be?"

"I don't know," Jason said after a few minutes. "Maybe Mom or Dad has some idea. It could be an animal. Or it could be some machine. You remember how strange that airplane sounded last summer that flew low over our house?"

"Yes, I had never heard anything like that before," Andy agreed. "It could be a machine of some kind. I guess we'll just have to keep checking out here and try to find it next time we hear it. When should we try to come out here again?"

"How about after supper?" Jason suggested.

"That sounds good to me, partner," Andy agreed. "Wouldn't it be neat if we could use a tape recorder and record the sound?"

Chapter Fifteen

After supper and doing the evening chores, the boys once again took a walk down the trail in their woods. However, whatever was making the bumping sound wasn't doing so now. "I guess we'll just have to keep checking back from time to time," Andy remarked, a little sadly.

When they returned to the house, they learned that Dad was going to take everyone for a drive. "I want to stop by and see Mrs. Joyner." Mrs. Joyner was a widow who attended their church. "She has been praying for us about the adoption for a long time. I would like for her to be one of the first of our friends to meet Matthew and Leah."

After their trip, it was time for Bible reading and prayer. The family all worked on their memory verses and then Dad read from the seventh chapter of Romans. "'For the good that I would I do not: but the evil which I would not, that I do.' What Paul is saying is that he doesn't do what he wants to do; instead he does what he hates to do. That sounds odd, doesn't it? If Paul really wanted to do something, why didn't he just do it? And if he really didn't want to do something, why did he go ahead and do it?" Dad let the question sink in.

"As Christians, our will is to obey God. Yet, we still have our old sinful bodies and our old sinful desires. Too often, we let our sinful nature take control of our lives. When we do that, we are no longer letting Christ be the Lord of our lives. Romans 7:14 calls that our 'carnal' nature." At the confused look on Ben's face, Dad decided to give some examples.

"The Bible says that I am to forgive people. I really wish I would forgive people. Yet, I find myself sometimes holding grudges a long time. In that case I'm not doing what I wish I would do. Instead, I'm doing what I hate to do. It really means that Satan has control of my life, not Jesus.

"There are many other examples we could think of as well. You may really wish you would obey your parents, but instead you disobey anytime you think you can get away with it. You may really wish you would be content, yet you lust after what you don't have. I really wish I would hunger for righteousness, yet I find myself instead focusing on the hunger of my belly. I really wish I would be humble, as Christ commanded, but find myself being proud of what I've done, instead. So, you see, it's easy to let Satan control your life."

Andy raised his hand and Dad called on him. "I know how to do things right. We need to pray and ask the Holy Spirit to help us do the right things and not do the wrong ones."

"That's right," Dad agreed. "It's only with the help of the Holy Spirit that we can do what God wants us to do. You need to understand that when you become a Christian, Satan has lost. So his goal now is to make sure you're carnal. At least if he can get you to do that, he can make you miserable and make your life useless for Christ. But remember what the Bible teaches us. James 4:7 says, 'Resist the devil and he will flee from you.' He will run away. If you will just resist him, with the power and help of the Holy Spirit, he will run from you. As we pray, let's all ask God to help us resist Satan and live for Jesus, instead."

Everyone got to their knees and prayed. After prayer, they sang the hymn *Lead On, O King Eternal*, which, as Dad explained, talked about fighting in the war we have with sin.

As the boys were settling down to sleep, Andy looked over at Matthew in his bed. Matthew seemed to be looking right at Andy. "Good night, Matthew," Andy said softly. Although he wasn't sure, he thought he saw Matthew grin at him. He didn't say anything however. *I wonder what he's thinking?* Andy thought. *I wonder if he misses Russia? I know I would miss this place terribly if I had to leave it.*

Andy thought more about Matthew and Leah. He tried to imagine what it would be like to leave his home. Andy knew he would feel very lonely. Why, just having Mom and Dad gone for several weeks had been terribly hard on Andy, and he even had his brothers and sister with him, not to mention his grandad. Andy began to think of ways in which he could make Matthew feel at home and how he could show the love of Christ to Matthew. He purposed in his heart to show compassion to Matthew and be kind to him in every way. With a feeling of light heartedness and determination to show kindness to Matthew, Andy went to sleep.

The next morning, Matthew seemed to be a little

less shy. He wanted to sit right next to Ben and smiled when Ben smiled at him. *He's going to be okay here*, thought Andy. Andy remembered to smile at Matthew all day long. He even offered Matthew his second cinnamon roll, a treasured possession to Andy.

After breakfast, Mom asked Jason to mop the basement floor before they would begin homeschooling. He enjoyed this job because he got to wear big rubber boots and get everything wet. "And try not to get everything down there wet this time," Mom instructed from the top of the stairs after Jason was already in the basement. "The last time it took several days for some of our boxes to dry out."

"Yes ma'am," Jason returned. "What are you going to do, Andy?" Andy had followed him down to the basement.

"I don't know," Andy replied. "What should I do?"

"Why don't you check on the Case of the Missing Tools?"

"That's a good idea!" Andy said, and was already sprinting up the stairs.

"It's back," Andy nearly shouted as he entered the house a few minutes later. "Hey, Dad, the Sawzall is back! Cathy, have you seen Dad?"

"I think he's in his study," she replied. "But Mom's rocking Leah, so you'll need to be quiet. What were you saying?"

"I'll tell you later," Andy answered in a lower voice. "I've got to tell Dad something important!"

Sure enough, Dad was in his study, working on some papers in front of him. Andy didn't interrupt,

but waited for Dad to turn around and address him.
"What is it, Andy?"

"The Sawzall is back, Dad! So are the chop saw
and the air compressor."

"What about the pneumatic stapler?"

"I forgot to look," Andy said. "And it's the
strangest thing. There is a note on top of the air
compressor that says, 'thanks'."

Dad stood up and stretched his back. "Well, at
least I'm glad they weren't stolen. But I wonder who
took them and brought them back? I've asked just
about every friend and neighbor I can think of. No
one has borrowed them and no one can think of
anyone doing any remodeling!"

"It's still a mystery, isn't it?" Andy asked.

"Yes, it is for me," Dad admitted. "Let's go take
a look at them." The two walked to the shop. Jason,
who had been sweeping in the basement, joined them.

"That's them all right." Dad looked the tools
over carefully. "And they don't look hurt or anything." He picked up the note from the air compressor. "It is written on the back of what looks like an
old calendar. Can't make out the month or year.
Also, it looks like it was written by a woman! Doesn't
it look like that to you?" he asked, handing the paper
to Andy.

"I don't know any men who can write that neatly
and . . . I guess you would call it fancy," assented
Andy. Jason agreed with the two of them.

Andy pulled out his notebook and began writing
down clues. "This mystery is certainly not over yet!"

They found the pneumatic stapler, but not where
it was supposed to be. In fact none of the tools were

in the right places. The air compressor and chop saw were very near the door while the stapler and Sawzall were on the workbench.

"If someone did borrow the tools and was just returning them, why didn't they put them back where they got them? And why didn't anyone come in and tell us they were returning them? And why can't we figure out who was borrowing them?" The questions came pouring out of the boys like water over a dam's spillway.

"We're going to have to do some more thinking about these clues," Jason noted.

"Yes, and I'm going to have to call Officer Stiles," Dad added. "At least they're back. Sure is a mystery, though."

The boys combed the shop for more clues while Dad went back to his office to call Mr. Stiles. Apparently the person entered the shop by the side door and placed the heavy air compressor and chop saw the first place they could. "That would make sense if it was a woman," Jason noted. "She wouldn't be as strong as Dad or able to carry it easily." He walked outside the door, then came back in. "Looks like she rolled the air compressor in," he observed. "There are little tracks in the dirt from the driveway to the shop door."

That was an interesting clue, and one that Andy immediately wrote in his notebook. Then he began rolling the air compressor back and forth to feel how heavy it was to move. "This is pretty heavy," he said. He rolled it to where it was supposed to stay and exclaimed, "Hey, what's this?" Reaching down, he picked up a small scrap of paper from the floor. "It must have been under the air compressor."

Both boys examined the piece of paper. It was a receipt from a local building supply store. "Looks like someone has been involved in a remodeling project," Andy commented. "They bought wood, glue, nails, and some trim. Hey, we shop at that store! I wonder if they would know who bought this stuff? Here's the date right at the top! Even the clerk's code is on there."

"Neat!" Jason exclaimed. "We could find the clerk and ask him who came in on that day and bought this stuff. Then we could solve the mystery!"

Andy was excited at first. However, the more he looked at the list, the less sure he was. "They sell lots of building supply things down there," he said. Looking at the receipt carefully, he added, "This has been over a month. With all the customers they have, they might not remember who bought these things, specifically."

"You're right of course," Jason agreed. "Let's see if there are any more clues or pieces of paper."

The boys looked carefully, but found no more receipts. Finally, they had to admit that the receipt was the only clue they had to go on. When they got to the house, they showed the receipt to Dad, who was impressed by their detective work.

"We'll have to check this out," he decided. "It's curiosity as much as anything right now. I'd really like to know who borrowed those tools."

"Can we go right now?" Jason asked hopefully.

"No, I'm afraid we can't go today," Dad said. "I have to train our new colt, and then we have to fix some fence later this afternoon. I'm still trying to catch up on things after our trip to Russia. And besides, I need to stay close to home today. Mom is going to have to spend a lot of time with Leah. She had another rough night last night. Mom thinks Leah is cutting some teeth, and she doesn't seem to feel well. Maybe tomorrow we can go to the building supply store in town."

Although the boys were a little disappointed, like most boys who have trouble being patient, they were still excited about the possible trip to town tomorrow. "Besides, today we get to do something we enjoy the most," Jason reflected. "Work with Dad on the farm!"

Chapter Sixteen

T he next morning proved to be overcast. The weather didn't depress the boys, however. They were so glad that Mom and Dad were back home that nothing else seemed important. Walking back to the house from doing morning chores, Andy noticed a movement at the woodpile.

"Hey, did you see that?" he asked. Jason and Ben hadn't. "It was over there. There it is again! Look!" He pointed to the bottom of the wood pile.

"I don't see anything," Ben complained.

"Keep looking, and you'll see . . . There it is!" Andy pointed quickly to a spot and his brothers squinted with visual concentration.

"I saw it!" Jason exclaimed.

Ben, however, still didn't see it. "What is it?"

"It looks like a weasel to me," Jason said. "It's got this cute little head . . . There! See it? It's right there."

Ben saw it and squealed. "How cute! Look at the way it keeps sticking its head out and looking at us."

"Say, I wonder if we can catch it," Andy offered. "Let's try."

The boys began moving logs to try to get to the bottom of the pile. Soon the weasel darted away from the woodpile and sought refuge in a nearby fire pit. This was really nothing more than a rock-lined circle where the family had cookouts and built campfires in the fall and winter.

"Now we can catch him easier!" Ben exclaimed.

The boys worked diligently, moving rocks and old half-burned logs trying to grab the weasel. However, he was very sleek and fast. The funny thing was that he was also very curious. He could have run away from the boys and never been seen again. Instead, he stayed right there, peeking out from behind a rock and scurrying from here to there. The boys were having so much fun that they didn't realize it was beginning to rain.

Mom opened the back door. "Boys, it's starting to rain."

"Mom, we found this weasel and we've almost caught him!" Jason stated. "Can we please stay here a minute and try to catch him?"

Mom smiled. That seemed like a perfectly reasonable request from a twelve-year-old boy. "As long as you don't bring it into the house. Do **not** bring him into the house." Hopefully by hearing it twice the message would sink in better. "And when you start getting wet you have to come right in."

"Yes ma'am," Andy responded for all the boys.

"Come on guys, let's move around so we won't get wet," Ben suggested. He started walking in a circle around the campfire pit.

However, the weasel soon tired of being chased and ran in the direction of the garage. He slipped into a crack and disappeared between the walls.

"I guess that's the end of trying to catch that weasel," Jason said. "He sure was cute, wasn't he?"

"Are you guys ready to head to town?" Dad

asked, walking into the garage. "I need to pick up some things at the supply house and we can check on that receipt you have."

"Yes sir!"

Soon the Nelson men, minus Matthew who wanted to stay home with Mom, were entering the building supply store in town. The smell of fresh popcorn filled the air. "Yummy!" exclaimed Ben. "Popcorn!"

A lady at the register, which was right next to the popcorn machine, heard Ben's comment. "Would you like some?" she asked him.

Ben looked at his dad, who just smiled and said, "Yes, I think it would be okay."

The lady handed Ben a small bag filled to the top with fresh popcorn. A few kernels fell to the ground and Ben reached over and picked them up. His hand was moving toward his mouth when Dad cautioned, "No, Ben. Don't eat the popcorn off the floor. Here, put it in this garbage can."

The lady laughed and asked the other boys if they wanted some also. After Dad grinned and nodded, the lady handed everyone a small bag. Dad moved toward the back of the store.

"I guess we'll pay for it when we check out, right Dad?" asked Andy anxiously.

"No, we don't have to pay for it," Dad responded. "It's free."

Andy just could not understand that. "How can they give it away for nothing? They would be losing money. Are you sure, Dad?"

"I'm sure, son. They give away popcorn because it makes us want to come into their store. Some stores don't give away popcorn, and this store hopes we will remember that and shop here when we need something. Does that make sense?"

Andy shook his head. "Someone has to pay for that popcorn."

Dad laughed. "You're right there, Andy. Someone does pay for it. I guess you could say that all of the customers of this store pay for it in a way, since we give them our money to buy things with. With some of that money, they buy popcorn."

"What about the people who don't like popcorn?" Jason asked. "Do they still have to pay their money for it?"

"Everyone pays the same prices for the same things in this store. They don't give you a discount just because you're not eating their popcorn, if that's what you mean."

Dad shopped for the items he needed and headed to the checkout. After paying for his purchases, he handed the clerk the receipt that Andy had found. "Are you by any chance the person who rung up this material?"

"Was there some mistake?" the clerk asked nervously.

"No, that's not why I'm asking," Dad replied kindly. "Actually, it's a rather long story. I'm just trying to find out who waited on this customer, that's all."

The lady seemed a little relieved, but not totally. She scanned the bottom of the receipt and read the numbers off. "Yes, that's my number. I must have done it. Are you sure I didn't make some kind of mistake? I'm pretty new here and I would hate to get into trouble of some kind."

"Don't worry," Dad assured her. "Whoever bought this material borrowed some tools of mine. I'm sure it's one of my friends and I'd just like to know which one."

The lady, more relieved now that Dad really was not going to get her into trouble, looked at the receipt again. "That's been over a month now. We have lots of customers come in here. I've had a number of customers buy that kind of trim. I notice that the person bought some paint. Do you have any idea what the color was? The receipt just says that it was a custom-mixed gallon of paint."

Dad looked unsure. Then he looked at the boys. "Any idea, guys?"

"No sir."

The clerk smiled and said kindly, "I'm sorry, sir. But I just can't remember all the customers who come in here and what they all buy. The reason I mentioned the paint color is that if we knew the color, then we could go to our computer and see who purchased it. We keep track of who buys what paint because people often want to buy more and they almost never remember the exact color they bought the first time."

"That makes sense," Dad said. "Well, guys, I guess we hit a dead-end after all. Thank you, ma'am."

"You're welcome. And thanks for shopping. Please come again. 'Bye boys!"

"Boy, we were so close." Jason was disappointed as they drove home.

"Who knows," Dad consoled. "I'm just sure that sooner or later we'll know who borrowed the tools. Surely we'll learn somehow."

"Yes, but we wanted to solve the mystery," Andy interjected. "Let's look for more clues when we get home," he said to Jason.

Dad interrupted. "I'm afraid when we get home that I have other work for you boys to do. We need to get the yard cleaned up for mowing. Plus, I have a list of other jobs we need to tackle today, if at all possible."

When they got home, the boys began cleaning up sticks and toys out of the yard. "Hey Jason, do you think that lady at the store told us everything she knew about our mystery person?"

"What do you mean, Andy?"

"Do you think she really knew more about who the customer was, but didn't tell us?"

Jason thought about that. "I don't want to think evil of anyone, but I sort of know what you mean. She seemed really nervous to me."

"That's what I mean," Andy agreed. "It could be because she was hiding something."

"It could also be because she was afraid that Dad was going to get her into trouble somehow. She said so herself."

"I know. It's just a feeling I had, that's all."

Chapter Seventeen

W hat should we do now?" Jason asked when they finished their work.

"Let's go to the shop one more time and search for clues about the Case of the Missing Tools," Andy suggested.

"I don't know, Andy. It seems like a waste of time to me. We've looked in there before. What new stuff do you think we'll find?"

"I don't know. You don't have to come if you don't want to," Andy replied. "I'll be glad to look myself."

"I think I'll let you. I want to ride my bike," Jason said honestly.

Andy walked toward the shop and opened the door. Now, where to begin looking? He looked all over and around the air compressor. He picked up the pneumatic stapler and turned it over and over in his hands. Then he had a thought. *What kind of staples were in the tool?* Quickly, he opened the chamber and several staples fell out. *So this is what size staple she was using!* He was very pleased with his discovery. He knew that Dad never kept staples inside the chamber when the stapler was in storage so these must be ones that the "borrower" had used.

They were long staples, about 1 ½ inches in length. *She must have been stapling something pretty thick to use a staple that long*, he thought.

He had a desire to run outside and tell Jason of his discovery. However, he had a stronger desire to show more self-control. That was unusual, but it was there nonetheless. Slowly he continued to look for clues on the stapler, but found nothing.

Turning to the Sawzall, he looked it over carefully. Most of the blades were still brand new, since the kit came with quite a number of blades and Dad hadn't used the tool much. He studied the used ones and tried to determine which blade the lady had used. Two blades showed wear, but no evidence presented itself as to which was the one she had used. *She might have even used a blade that she bought herself*, he thought. Many people who borrowed tools did that, so as not to ruin or dull the owner's blades.

He was about to walk out of the shop when he remembered the chop saw. He walked over to it and just stared at it. *Nothing looks unusual to me*, he thought, turning to go. Then he saw it. It was small, probably not over one inch long and 1/4 inch wide. But there it was. With hands trembling, he reached down and picked it up. Carefully, he studied it and turned it over in his hand. Then he raced out of the shop, forgetting his desire to display lots of self-control.

"Jason, look what I've found!" he exclaimed when he found his brother. He held out two items for his brother to see.

"A few staples," Jason said, turning them over in his hand. "Out of the staple gun?" When Andy nodded, he said, "Good job, Andy! Now we have a better feel for what she used it for. Must have been something thick."

"Right," Andy agreed. "But this is the best clue," he said, handing Jason the other small clue.

"A tiny piece of wood?" Jason didn't get the connection. "How will that help us?"

Andy was so excited he could hardly talk. "I found it in one of the grooves of the chop saw." He waited for his brother to catch on.

Jason was having trouble understanding the significance of the wood chip. "And?"

"Look at it closely, partner, and tell me everything about it that you see."

Jason did as instructed. "It's a small piece of wood. Boy, that would make a very painful splinter! Let's see, it looks like pine." He smelled the wood. "Yes, I would say it's not oak, for sure. And it's been painted on one side a blue color." Jason suddenly almost exploded. "Hey, it's blue! That must be the color that the lady painted her wood. Now we can check it at the building supply store and see what kind of color it is! That will probably tell us who the lady is!"

"Yes!" Andy exclaimed. "Let's go tell Dad."

The two rushed into the house and almost knocked Cathy down. "Sorry, Cathy," Jason apologized. "I'm sorry, I was just coming in to find Dad. Do you know where he is?"

"He's out on a trail ride," Cathy answered. "He's trying to train one of the new horses. I don't expect him back for several hours."

"Thanks," Jason said, and the two boys walked back outside. "What do we do while we're waiting for Dad?"

Midnight Sky

The boys finally decided to go to their office and talk about the Case of the Missing Tools. "Even though we have the piece of wood, how can we be sure what color it is?" Jason asked.

"It's dark blue," Andy said matter-of-factly.

"I know," Jason agreed. "But there must be about a million different blues. What if their computer has a lot of people who bought blue paint that day?"

"I didn't think of that," Andy said. "I guess we'll just have to wait and see when we get there." He then changed subjects. "What about The Case of the Strange Bump?"

"We don't have any more clues," Jason said. "I suppose we should try and get back out there and listen again. Maybe we can do it after lunch. Let's go and talk to Dad about what we've found in the shop. Okay?"

Andy and Jason went outside by the barn to wait for their dad to appear from the trail. Finally, they heard the snorting of a young horse and then Dad and his mount came into view from the woods.

"You boys stand back," Dad directed. "This horse is a little skittish yet and I don't want you to get hurt. I also don't want you to scare him so that I get hurt."

The boys obeyed promptly. But the horse acted fine and walked into the barn, led by Dad's firm pull on the lead rope. After the horse was back in his stall, Jason asked the question that was weighing on the boys' minds.

"Dad, do you think we can go back to the building supply house again soon? We found something that might solve the Case of the Missing Tools."

"What did you find?" asked Dad, quite interested.

"This," answered Andy, handing Dad the piece of painted wood.

"Well, look at that! It's painted blue. Think this is our mystery color, guys?"

"Yes sir. We found that on the chop saw, Dad."

Dad looked at his watch. "It can't be today, boys. I'm sorry but I just have too much to do. We'll try to go there soon, okay?"

"Dad, do you think if we just called and told them that it was dark blue that they could look it up for us in their computer?" Jason offered.

Dad thought about that a minute. Finally, he shook his head. "No, son. I'd rather not do that. This is a mystery to us, but it won't really help them at all, so I would hate to tie them up on the phone about it. No, I would feel better about going down in person and asking them. We'll do it soon."

"I hope so," Andy said.

Chapter Eighteen

When the boys returned to the house, they found Ben in the basement doing something with ropes. Matthew was standing by the washing machine, staring at his big brothers.

"Hi, what's up?" Andy asked in a friendly voice.

"We're playing," Ben said.

"Well, it looks like **you're** playing, anyway," Jason smiled. "Is Matthew going to help you?"

"Sure," Ben replied confidently. "We're going to be workers for the electric company. Some lines are down and we have to fix them. Right, Matthew?"

Matthew just kept staring at his oldest brothers and didn't offer any answer.

Jason and Andy went upstairs and started on their math lesson. Andy worked through some hard fraction problems, while Jason was busy trying to divide decimals.

"Fractions are hard," Andy said, putting down his pencil after erasing yet another mistake.

"Just wait until you get into decimals," Jason commented. Andy stood up, stretched, and walked over to look at Jason's math homework. He whistled low.

"That looks hard to me," he said, in awe of his brother's ability to work such difficult-looking problems. "How do you do it with all of those periods everywhere?"

"Those are called 'decimal points.' Actually, it's not that hard. You just have to make sure you keep those decimal points all lined up." Jason looked over at Andy's homework, and said, a little confidentially, "With decimals, you never have to find a least common denominator."

Andy was excited by that piece of news. "Really? Maybe I could just start doing decimals now."

Jason wasn't hopeful. "No, I think you will still have to learn fractions first. Think about all the times that Dad uses fractions every day. He uses them when he's measuring wood to cut, when he needs to use a socket wrench, and just lots of times. No, I think you better keep working until you 'master fractions,' like Mom always calls it."

"Andy, can you run to the basement and bring up another roll of paper towels?" Mom called from the kitchen.

"Yes ma'am." Andy was glad for the diversion. He walked down the basement steps and turned the corner into the room set aside for washing clothes and storing supplies. He wasn't really paying attention to where he was walking and almost got strangled on a low-hanging rope. Taking in the scene, he got a smile on his face.

There stood Matthew and Ben in the middle of a confusing array of strings, still playing "electric company workers."

"Hello sir!" Ben called out. "Stand back, please. We've got a few lines down here and I wouldn't want you to get hurt."

Matthew was smiling. Both boys were wearing winter mittens, which looked a little funny since both were also wearing short sleeve shirts and thin pants. They had on baseball caps turned backwards, which were probably substituting for hard hats in some way. Ben reached down and ever so carefully picked up one end of a piece of string. "This has 15 million volts in it, so stand back! I'm not afraid, though, because I have Matthew here. He can handle any wires and not get hurt. He's so brave. Here, Matthew! Put that on that pole over there! Good! Didn't get shocked? Good! Now we're making progress, men." Ben seemed to be directing a rather large force of electrical repair workers.

Andy looked at the imaginary electrical wires. They were made up of an assortment of things: an old bow string from Dad's hunting bow, three ancient shoe strings, one long roller skate string, and a whole host of girls' pink and purple hair ribbons. These were all tied together to make the 'main' circuit, apparently, and went from the pipe behind the washing machine to the furnace door handle. There were other imaginary electrical lines running in other directions as well. Most of these, however, were just old pieces of baling twine.

"Well, you guys are busy!" Andy said, enthusiastically. "Are you getting ready for someone to build a new subdivision or something?"

"No," Ben answered in a deep voice, trying to sound very masculine. "It's like that thing near the church with all those wires running everywhere."

Andy thought for a second. "You mean the substation?"

"Yes," Ben replied. "We're having to do some work because there was a tornado that came ripping through here a few minutes ago. Tore down lots of lines. Watch out! Here comes another one!" He ducked quickly and Matthew did the same thing, giggling. It was obvious that tornados were pretty common in the basement this morning.

"Well, that messed up some more electrical lines!" Ben said huskily. "You all right there, Matthew?"

Matthew rose from a crouching position, grinning, but saying nothing. He handed some baling twine to Ben.

"Yes, guess we better put this one up again. Been knocked down twenty times in the last hour. This is hard work. But we're glad to do it," he continued in his husky voice. "It's for the children that we work so hard, you know. They need electricity so their moms can make them lunch. Well, got to work now, see you!" With that Ben turned and started tying the rope to a nail by the door. Matthew reached down and picked up another of Cathy's old hair ribbons.

I'm glad Matthew is finally feeling a little less scared of us, Andy thought.

"Andy, where are you? And where are those paper towels?" Mom called from upstairs.

"I'm sorry. Coming, Mom," Andy called up. "See you later, men."

Ben was too busy "saving" lunches for the neighborhood children to answer. He just saluted and kept on tying his knots. Matthew smiled shyly at Andy.

After finishing their math and eating lunch, the older boys walked outside for a breath of fresh air.

Midnight Sky

They just naturally made their way to the path through the woods.

Andy and Jason walked slowly, stopping from time to time, trying to pick up the strange sound again. The Case of the Strange Bump needed some more clues if it was going to be solved.

Jason stopped and seemed disappointed.

"What's wrong?" Andy asked quietly.

"I forgot to see if we could bring a tape recorder out here with us," Jason said.

"Oh well, we have our ears," Andy tried to console his brother. "We'll just have to listen carefully and remember what we hear."

The two continued walking again. Finally, they came to the tree they had been near when they heard the sound for the first time. "Should we stop here and just sit a while?" suggested Andy.

Jason nodded and dropped to the ground. He pulled out his notebook, and turned to the page with notes about The Case of the Strange Bump. Looking at his watch, he recorded the time, then leaned back and rested on the soft bed of leaves. Andy did essentially the same things.

Sitting still for a long period of time isn't hard for many people. But Andy and Jason were young boys who liked action, not boys who liked to just sit around. After a while, Jason stood up and stretched his legs. "I guess we're not going to hear it today," he remarked. "Let's head back to the house."

Andy agreed, and the pair started back toward their farm. Then it happened. "Bump . . . bump. . bump . bump, bump." Without saying anything, Andy pointed in one direction and looked at Jason with a questioning look on his face. Jason shrugged his shoulders as though unsure of the direction the sound had come from. Slowly the boys moved in the direction that Andy had pointed.

Maybe the boys' movement caused the sound-maker to be frightened. Maybe the sound-maker wasn't going to make any more sounds today anyway. At any rate, the bump sound didn't happen again. Finally, the boys had to admit that it seemed over for today.

"That's weird," Jason said, as they began talking out loud again. "The last time we heard it, it made the sounds a bunch of times. Today it only did it once."

"Maybe," Andy said. "Or maybe the sounds have been made all day and we just happened to hear the last one."

"That's true," Jason agreed. "What did you write in your notes, Andy?"

"Well, I still agree it sounds kind of like a bowling ball. But it also sounded a little bit like someone chopping a tree down."

"You heard someone chopping a tree?"

"No, not exactly," Andy said. "But let's say that someone has cut a great big heavy tree. The sound I heard sounded like that tree thumping as it hit the ground and then thumping faster as it hit it again and again until it bounced to a stop."

"But wouldn't you have heard limbs and leaves rustling as they struck the ground?"

Andy thought about that a minute. "You're right," he reluctantly agreed. "I guess it sounds more like a heavy telephone pole being dropped to the ground."

Midnight Sky

"I know what you mean though," Jason responded. "Maybe that's why it sounds a little like a bowling ball falling to me. It is definitely something heavy, and it sounds like it's hitting the ground hard."

The two wrote more in their notebooks. "Hey, you know what it sounds like a little bit?" Jason said. "Sort of like someone trying to start an engine. What we've been calling a 'bump' could actually be a 'put', you know like an engine trying to start with 'put . . . put. . put . put, put.' And the more the person tries to start it, the closer he comes to actually getting it going. That's why the 'put's' get closer together."

Andy wasn't so sure of this one. "Then why don't we hear the engine actually start? And besides, who is trying to start an engine in our woods? Wouldn't we know if someone was doing that?"

"Maybe we would, and maybe we wouldn't," Jason replied, looking around him in the woods. "You know there are lots of places that people can get access to our land. Why it's even possible that someone is trying to start a chain saw or some other tool. And maybe they're going to use it to cut down some of our good trees. You remember that Dad said we have some pretty valuable black walnut trees."

That thought sobered Andy a little. It was possible. And Dad had even told the boys that some trees were worth over $2000 just the way they were. Those trees could be used to cut expensive walnut veneers because they were so healthy and didn't have many limbs or curves.

"I think we better tell Dad about it and see what he says," Andy suggested.

"I agree!" The two boys hurried to find Dad.

Chapter Nineteen

That's very interesting," Dad remarked after listening to the boys tell the latest clues of the Case of the Strange Bump. "There are people who steal trees, especially trees that are as valuable as some we have. Now, you say you hear the bumping sound, but then it stops when you start walking toward it?"

"We don't really know if it is stopping because we're walking in that direction, or if it would just stop on its own," Jason admitted. "Also, the sound isn't always out there. Sometimes we walk and listen and never hear anything."

"That makes it more difficult to solve," Dad said. "It's like when the transmission on my truck kept acting up. Since it only made the sound sometimes, it was almost impossible for the mechanic to find out what was wrong with the truck. Of course, it never made the sound when I was at the repair shop, only when I was by myself on some lonely stretch of road," he smiled.

"Are you worried about your trees?" Andy asked.

"Not really," Dad answered truthfully. "It would take some pretty heavy machinery to come in and take them out. I think we would hear them even from the farm here. Also, we would certainly be able to see their tracks. You boys didn't see any unusual tracks did you?"

"No sir," Jason admitted. "I'm glad it's probably

not someone taking out our good trees. I would hate to think of someone stealing them."

"It's about time for supper," Mom announced. "Jason, you need to set the table, please. And Andy, would you please find Ben and Matthew and have them get washed up?"

Andy walked to the basement, but didn't find the boys. He did find evidence that they had been there, however. In fact, they had been quite busy. Now two whole areas of the basement were covered with "electrical lines." It was almost impossible to walk through the rooms without getting caught. *Boy, they sure must have had fun,* he thought. He remembered back to times when he and Jason had done this same kind of thing. They had spent hours pretending to be just about everything you could imagine. He remembered when they were plumbing contractors, installing the Panama Canal. He laughed out loud as he thought of that. *Imagine plumbers building the Panama Canal.* Of course, they had also been cowboys, road construction workers, and roofing contractors.

Andy looked in the shop, but the boys weren't there. As he was walking toward the barn, he saw a plastic toy saw lying on the ground. Picking it up, he thought back to many years ago, when he and Jason had pretended to be surgeons using this very same saw. Smiling, he remembered how each had worn one of Dad's old white dress shirts, put on backwards with the sleeves rolled up. Cathy had helped them make surgeons' hats out of pieces of white paper. Each hat had a big red cross on the front of it. He could almost still hear the conversations.

"Cathy, do you need some surgery? We are

running a special today. Your first surgery is free. And the next one is half-priced!"

"Yes, I'll come have surgery, but you can't hurt me or anything."

"I won't hurt you. Here, come in here. This is my assistant, Dr. Jason. Dr. Jason, this is our patient!"

"Thank you for coming, patient. Please lay down and this won't take long at all. What kind of surgery should we do, Dr. Andy?"

"We are going to remove her leg and most of her teeth. Yes, I'm sorry, patient, but we must!" Andy said, as Cathy started to get up. "You want to be well, don't you?"

"Okay, please be very still. Dr. Jason, please hold that flashlight still," Andy said, beginning to use his plastic saw. "There, now the leg's off . . . oops, Dr. Jason, I think I took the wrong one off . . . Yes, I sure did. My, I'm getting forgetful." Andy wiped his forehead with a handkerchief. "Will you sew it back on while I pull the other one off? Thank you, Dr. Jason."

Cathy was giggling. "Am I well?"

"No, we have to give you gas. It will help you sleep."

"I thought I should get that before you took off my legs."

"We could. But we don't have to use so much this way . . . There, now that you've had the gas, I need to tell you that it may make you very sick . . . I'm sorry, but that's the way it goes. Next!" Jason left the room looking for more patients, while Andy picked up a copy of a medical journal, that was actually a flyer for a house painting company. "I have to read these things so I know how to do the latest surgery. All of us doctors do this," he said, crossing his legs. "Ah, here's another patient now... "

And so, Jason and Andy had continued their medical practice for several days, before moving on to pretend totally different things. Andy remembered those days with pleasure. It had been so much fun. And now, it was fun to see Matthew and Ben pretending in the same ways.

He finally found the boys behind the barn and together they all headed toward the house for supper.

Mom had made spaghetti, salad, and fresh French bread for supper. The kitchen and dining area gave off a most delightful aroma. After prayer, Jason, Andy, and Ben began eating with their usual gusto. Matthew seemed to enjoy the French bread, although he didn't care for the spaghetti much.

"Mom, can I have Matthew's spaghetti?" Ben asked.

Mom smiled. "No, I think it would be better for Matthew to learn to eat the foods we have." She looked a little concerned. "He needs to eat more than just bread. As time goes on, I know he will learn to like more of the kinds of food I make. Until then, we'll make sure he doesn't feel like he needs to give us his food to eat." Matthew just smiled at Mom and continued eating his slice of bread.

After supper and chores, Dad thought it would be fun to take a little drive on their property in his pickup. All of the boys jumped in the back with smiles on their faces.

"This is fun!" Ben announced to Matthew. "Just wait and see!"

Dad drove slowly through one hay field and onto a small path cut through the woods. The boys had to duck to miss low-lying branches. Dad watched them from the window of the cab, making sure everyone was having fun and being safe.

"Let's pretend we're going to a secret hideaway for persecuted Christians in Vietnam," Andy suggested. "They live deep, deep in the jungle, to avoid getting into trouble with the communists who would arrest them if they caught them worshiping Jesus."

That sounded exciting, so Jason and Ben played along. Matthew smiled, but didn't seem to totally understand what was going on.

"We need to be very quiet for a few minutes," Jason half-whispered. "We're about to pass a village that has some people in it who aren't very friendly to Christians. If they hear us, they might come out and ask us where we are going."

Everyone was silent for a few seconds. Then Andy spoke up. "That was a close call. Did you see how that man came out of his hut and looked right in our direction?"

"Yes, but he didn't see us!" Jason exclaimed. "God protected us."

"I sure hope we get there soon," Ben offered. "Holding all of these Bibles is getting pretty heavy."

"Well, you can put them down if you need to. Here, you can put them over here with these shovels and water purifiers we are taking in. Say, I hope these radios still work when we get there. This has been a pretty bumpy road today," Andy observed, as the truck went over a large bump in the path.

"Look, there's a man waving to us," Ben said.

"What? . . . You want what? . . . Sure, here you go," he said, pretending to toss something to the imaginary person addressing him.

"What was that all about?" asked Jason.

"The man wanted a Bible and a jug of apple juice," Ben answered. "I'm happy that we had both to give him."

"We're slowing down," Jason noticed. "We must be about there. Remember, don't bring out any Bibles until we're sure there are no spies here."

The truck came to a stop and Dad stepped out of the cab. "I'll just be a minute," Dad commented. "I need to make sure the bee hives we set back near this hay field look okay." With that he walked about 150 feet from the truck.

"That man said that the coast was clear," Andy offered. "We had better share these Bibles and supplies with the people very quickly and be on our way. You never know when one of the authorities might show up." The boys pretended to unload materials and carry them behind a tree. Matthew watched all of this with a look of wonder on his face. He didn't understand what the boys were doing or why.

"Quick!" Ben stated in alarm. "Back in the truck, men. One of the leaders is heading this way. Everyone drop down out of sight."

Dad walked back to the truck. He had caught a drift of the boys' conversation while driving in, since he had his window down and he was driving slowly. He decided to join their action. "I'm sure there were Christians here just a little while ago," he said out loud, pretending to be talking to a group of men. "If we could only find them, we could arrest them and destroy their truck and provisions. That would put a stop to these Bibles being delivered back here to the deep jungle tribes. And then maybe we could find the rest of the Christians that are left back here. We've got to put an end to Christianity in our land!"

The boys listened as Dad continued talking. It was interesting because he was being so realistic in the way he was talking.

Dad suddenly slammed the truck with his hand several times. "Bang! Bang!" was the sound. "Stop, comrade!" he said to an imaginary person. "We must not shoot into the bushes unless we know exactly where they are. Your gun may have just frightened them off!"

That sobered the boys a lot. It had seemed exciting at first, but now it was getting serious. Andy popped up from the bed of the truck. "Dad, we're back here. I'm ready to stop pretending."

"Me too," Jason agreed. "It's getting a little too real."

Ben didn't want to stop, but sat up when his brothers did. "Are we back to safety?" he asked.

"Dad, that was scary when you hit the truck, making it sound like someone shot into the bushes."

"I'm sorry, Jason," Dad said gently. "I would never do anything to frighten you. Never! I wasn't trying to scare you. I was just trying to go along with the scenario that I thought you had set up."

Jason thought about that a moment. "Yes, I know you were, Dad. It's just that it was so real. For a minute there, I felt a little bit like it was all really happening or something."

"Me too," Andy admitted. "Dad, it would be

awful to have to live that way, wouldn't it? I mean, having to hide and always be afraid that the police might find you and arrest you just because you love Jesus would be terrible."

"You've learned an important lesson," Dad said. "We read about the persecuted church a lot, but somehow it doesn't always seem so real, does it? But then when we do something like this, you realize that not only could it happen, but that it is in fact happening."

"Yes!" Jason agreed. "My heart was pounding."

"I'm really sorry, guys. I honestly didn't mean to frighten you," Dad said, rubbing Jason's shoulders. "It is serious business, isn't it? Even as we are speaking, right now, there are many, many brothers and sisters in Christ feeling just the way you felt a minute ago. And not because someone was pretending, either." Dad looked at his boys with compassion. "Let's pray for them right now." Dad knelt down beside the truck and prayed. "Dear God, thank You that You have helped us see a little of what it must be like to be a persecuted Christian. Please be with our brothers and sisters in Christ right now, wherever they are, whatever they are experiencing. Help them to feel Your presence and feel secure in Your care. Please help us to know how we can help them. Use our gifts to aid wherever possible. And please, Father, help us not to ever forget them. Thank You that You have protected us, so far, from any persecution like that. But prepare us for any that might come in the future. We praise Your Name because we know that You will be victorious in all ways in the end. Help us to be strong. In Jesus' Name we pray, amen."

As Dad rose to his feet, Jason asked, "Dad, do you think it could really happen here?"

Dad got a serious look on his face. "Jason, it could happen anywhere. Down through history there have been people who thought things would go on forever just like they were going right then. But then something caused everything to change. Yes, it could happen here in America. I'm not saying that it will. Only God knows that. I'm just saying that it could."

That was a very sobering thought for the boys, and wasn't the first time they had heard of this possibility. But somehow, it had always seemed so unlikely.

"I'm glad we send help to those who are being persecuted," Andy said. "I'm glad there is an organization like Voice of the Martyrs and other ones like it who are trying to help those in need. I would really want some help if I was being persecuted."

"Exactly," Dad agreed. "It's easier to see how needy someone can be when you're needy yourself. We should pray that more Christians in free parts of the world will heed the call to help their brothers and sisters in Christ." Dad stepped back into the truck and started it up. "All ready back there?" he called.

"Yes sir," came the voices. Dad slowly drove back to the farm.

By the time they got back, it was time to get washed up and ready for bed. At Bible time that night, Dad related the boys' experience in the woods to Cathy and Mom. "We all have to be ready for whatever the future holds," Dad said. "Like I said, I don't know that it will ever happen in the U.S. Yet, there is no guarantee that things will remain the same. We can thank God that He always stays the same and is always there for us when we call on Him.

"That reminds me of a story I read yesterday. A number of years ago, a man in Chicago learned that both of his nieces had died with diphtheria within twenty-four hours of each other. He loved them very much and was extremely saddened by this news. God helped him to meditate upon Psalm 46. Here, let me read it." Dad read the Psalm, then continued.

"As he thought about those verses, he felt led to put some words down on paper and music to go with them. At the double-funeral for his nieces, that song was sung for the first time. The words went like this:

There is a place of quiet rest
Near to the heart of God,
A place where sin cannot molest,
Near to the heart of God.

O, Jesus, blest Redeemer,
Sent from the heart of God,
Hold us who wait before Thee
Near to the heart of God.

There is a place of comfort sweet
Near to the heart of God,
A place where we our Savior meet,
Near to the heart of God.

There is a place of full release
Near to the heart of God,

A place where all is joy and peace,
Near to the heart of God.
        (by Cleland Boyd McAfee)

"So, you see, that no matter what happens to us, whether it be persecution or the death of a loved one, or whatever, God is there for us. He is, as the Psalmist wrote, ' . . . a very present help in trouble . . .' As we pray tonight, let's ask God to help us remember that fact. And then to never be afraid. After all, if God be for us, who can be against us?" The family knelt in prayer. Then they sang the hymn *Near to the Heart of God*, with a more complete understanding of its significance and meaning.

As they settled down for bed, Andy remarked, "You know, I was afraid in the woods today. But after what Dad said tonight, I don't think I would be so afraid."

Jason agreed. "I would hope that I would trust in God. It would help if I could just remember what Dad said."

"I think that's one reason we memorize Bible verses," Andy said. "That way, when we are afraid, they pop into our heads almost automatically. At least, they have a better chance of doing that than if we didn't know them. I'm going to work extra hard on learning Bible verses. You never know when we might need them."

Chapter Twenty

T he next morning, after schoolwork was finished, Andy and Jason asked permission to go outside for a while.

"You've worked hard this morning," Mom said, studying their compositions. "Okay, but remember to be back in time for lunch."

Stepping into the bright sunshine, the boys felt refreshed almost at once. "Let's go and see if we can learn anything else about The Case of the Strange Bump," Jason suggested. "Say, why don't you go ask Dad if it would be okay if we borrowed his tape recorder?"

Andy thought about that for a minute. "Well. . . why don't you ask him, Jason? I mean you're more grown up than me. Maybe he'll let you borrow it."

Jason suddenly acted grown up. "Okay, I will." He was back in a few minutes. "Dad said it would be okay if we promised to take good care of it and brought it back in the house every time after we used it."

"Great!" Andy enthused. Then looking down at Jason's empty hands, he asked, "But where's the tape player? Why didn't you bring it with you?"

"That's what I was going to tell you. We can use it. But it runs on batteries and Dad doesn't have any batteries to fit it. He said we never need batteries, and so if we want to use it outside, we would need to buy some."

"How much do they cost?" Andy asked.

"I don't know, but Dad said the tape player needs six of them."

"Couldn't we just buy one or two batteries? We aren't going to use it a long time, you know."

"No, we have to fill up the whole thing with batteries," Jason said. "It's like that train set we had. It had to have five batteries. Remember the time we tried to run it on only one battery because that's all we had? We thought that it would be okay, just maybe run slowly. Well, it didn't run at all."

"You're right, and I remember that Dad said batteries cost a lot of money, too. I guess we can check on them the next time we go to the hardware store. How much money do you have?"

"Not much," Jason responded. "I still have a little money that Aunt Ruth sent me for my birthday. How about you?"

"I don't have anything, except that silver dollar that Mr. Mashburn gave me for memorizing those Bible verses," Andy said. "I guess we'll just have to see how much they cost. Let's go out to the woods now, anyway, and see if we can solve the mystery. It would be nice to solve it for free, instead of having to buy batteries!"

The two walked down the path into the woods. "Want to go to the same spot?" Jason asked, breaking the silence.

"Why don't we go in that direction?" Andy asked, pointing. "Maybe we will seem closer and be able to tell better what's going on." The boys settled down and began quietly eating several biscuits that were left from breakfast. Mom had okayed this and they were glad they had something interesting to do while waiting for the sound to "appear." They didn't have to wait long.

"Bump . . . bump. . bump . bump, bump."

"Do you think it could be someone giving a signal to someone else?" Andy asked. "It could even be that someone is trying to signal us, although I doubt it. We hear it but don't have a clue where to go or what to do."

"If so, it's a pretty strange signal to be sending," Jason replied honestly.

"Remember we read how Indians had all kinds of signals they used to communicate with each other? The white men usually didn't even know an Indian was anywhere near. But the Indians were able to tell each other all kinds of things just by using different sounds."

That gave Andy an idea. "Why didn't I think of it before?"

"What?" Jason asked.

"Why don't we try to recreate the sound ourselves? Then it would be easier for others to help us figure out what is causing it."

"Yes! That's a good idea," Jason said enthusiastically. "What can we use? I know. Maybe we can make the sound by using an old pipe. If we thunked it on the ground it might make the same sound."

"Let's go try it!" suggested Andy, jumping up. Both boys headed toward the farm. But as they were walking quickly, "Bump . . . bump. . bump . bump, bump" echoed through the woods.

"I can hardly wait to figure out what is making that sound!" Jason said.

When they got to the house, the boys checked with Mom and Dad to make sure they didn't have any chores to do. Then they ran to the barn to find some old pipe. "Here's a good one!" Jason picked up an old water pipe that was about two feet long. Quickly, he thumped it on the ground.

"Bemp . . . bemp" was the sound it made. "Humph, not the right sound," he decided. "It's too high."

Andy picked up a piece of old drain pipe. Dropping it to the ground, it made a sound like "Boomp... boomp." "Well, this one makes a sound that is too low." The boys had fun rummaging through the barn trying to find small pieces of pipe to test.

Before long, there was a collection of five different sized pipes on the ground. Each made a slightly different sound. The boys experimented and found that they could lay the pipes in order from a higher sound to a lower sound. "Hey, we're making a musical instrument!" Jason said happily.

Cathy walked toward the barn, carrying a bowl of old carrots to feed to the horses. "Hi, guys. What are you doing?"

"Listen to this." Picking up a stick, Andy struck each pipe in order from the fattest to the skinniest. "Isn't that neat?"

"If you say so, Andy," Cathy said with a smile on her face. "But what are all of the pipes really for?"

"We're trying to recreate the sound that we hear in the woods," Jason answered. "We found that all of these pipes make a different sound."

Midnight Sky

"That's right," Cathy nodded. "They all have a different pitch. Pitch is how high or low the sound is. A low pitch is like this one," she said, striking one of the biggest pipes. "And this one has a high pitch. Do you know why they sound different?"

The boys didn't and Cathy patiently explained. "When you strike one of those pipes, sound waves are given off. They are kind of like the ripples you see when you toss a pebble in a still pond. Think of sound waves as the air vibrating. The more it vibrates, the higher the pitch."

Andy still looked confused.

"Think of this," Cathy started again, trying to find another way to explain the concept. "I've seen you boys attach a piece of cardboard to your bikes so it would hit the bicycle spokes and make a noise."

"I don't think that hurts anything," Andy said, defensively.

"I'm sure it doesn't," Cathy assured. "But the point I'm trying to make is this. The faster you turn the wheel, the more rapidly the cardboard is going to vibrate back and forth. Right?"

"Yes," Andy agreed.

"Well, when you are pedaling fast and the cardboard is vibrating fast, the sound it makes is a high pitch. When you slow down, and the cardboard is not vibrating very fast, the sound it makes is a lower pitch. Does that make sense?"

"Sure," Jason said. "Andy, it's like when we turn the fan on in the summer. When we turn it on low, it makes a low pitched sound. When we turn it on high, it makes a higher pitched sound. I wonder if that's how a piano works?"

135

"That's right," Cathy praised. "Low sounds on the piano are made because the string doesn't vibrate very much. I remember reading that the string for the lowest note on a piano only vibrates about thirty times each second. The strings for the highest note on a piano vibrate about 4,000 times a second!"

"So, when I strike this pipe, it makes a low kind of sound because it isn't vibrating very much." Andy demonstrated this law of sound. "Now when I strike this pipe, it makes a much higher sound, or pitch as you call it, because it is vibrating a lot more. Right?"

"Right," Cathy said.

"Thanks! That's interesting." Andy was ready to put this new information to practical use. "Cathy, we need to make a sound that is lower than this one," he tapped one pipe, "but higher than this one," he said, tapping another pipe. "What should we look for?"

"The pitch is determined by lots of things. Like how big around the pipe is on the outside and how big it is on the inside, and how long it is," Cathy stated. Examining the pipes, she finally concluded, "I'd say you need a pipe that is just a little more narrow than this one."

"Thanks," Jason replied. "I think I know where some more pipes are, Andy." The two boys raced to the back of the barn. For comparison, Jason carried the pipe that Cathy had suggested was a little too wide.

Sure enough there were several more pipes laying there. Looking them over, Jason picked up a pipe and compared it to the one in his hand. "No, just a little too wide, still. How about that one over there, Andy? No, not that one. Yes, that's the one."

Andy picked up the pipe and thunked it on the ground. "Bump . . . bump."

"That's it!" Jason exclaimed with excitement. "Cathy was right!"

Both boys took turns dropping the pipe on the ground, trying to make it give the exact sound that they had heard in the woods. "This is great!" Andy said. "Let's go let Dad hear it and see if he knows what could be making the sound."

In the house, they found Dad doing some paperwork at his desk. They were silent until Dad finally put down his pencil and asked, "How can I help you young men?"

"Dad, we can make the sound that we hear in the woods!" Andy informed.

"That's nice, guys," he said, turning back to his papers. "Just don't make a lot of noise in the house. Your mom has a headache this morning."

"Dad, don't you see? We can make the sound so you can tell us if you know what it is," Jason explained.

"Now why didn't I think of that?" Dad asked, with a smile on his face. "But let's go outside, okay?"

When they were outside, Jason asked, "Andy, do you want to do the honors?"

"Thank you," said Andy with dignity. He dropped the pipe on the ground.

"Bump . . . bump. . bump."

"It's a bump all right," Dad agreed. "Let me think a second." Dad seemed to be in deep thought. "It's no use," he finally admitted. "I can't think of anything that would make that sound. It does sound a lot like a bowling ball, as you described earlier. I'm sorry, guys. Maybe the sound will ring a bell for Mom or Cathy or even Ben. If I think of anything I'll let you know."

"Thanks, Dad," Jason said. The boys dropped the pipe for everyone else in their family, but no one seemed to know what could make such a sound.

"Well, it looks like we're back to square one," Andy admitted. "Maybe we should look into buying those batteries after all. It could be that someone would know what the sound is if they heard it just like we do."

"Maybe so," Jason agreed. "We'll look into buying batteries the next time we shop with Mom."

Chapter Twenty-one

On Saturday, Andy and Jason took another walk in the woods to see if they could learn more about The Case of the Strange Bump. For some reason, however, the sound didn't occur. Walking back toward the barn, they were discussing the facts about the case. Just then, a pickup pulled into the Nelson driveway.

"It's Mr. Kyle," Jason noticed.

Mr. Kyle, Andy thought. *Now, what is it I remember about him?* "Oh, I remember," Andy said out loud. "He said he was going to borrow Dad's air compressor sometime soon. Remember? When Dad was in Russia and we were trying to find out if anyone had borrowed his tools?"

"I remember," Jason said. "Let's go see if we can help."

Dad and Mr. Kyle were already talking. "No, I never did find out who borrowed the tools," Dad was saying. "Doesn't really matter, I don't suppose. Probably just a friend and I'll find out soon enough."

"Still, it seems strange that no one has even thanked you for letting them borrow them," Mr. Kyle remarked. "Even if I just walked in and got the tools without asking, which I would never do you know, I would at least say thanks when I brought them back."

"Our mystery tool-borrower did write a note to

that effect," Dad remembered.

"Yes, but I heard that he didn't call. Did he?"

"No. And actually, the handwriting on the note seemed to be more like that of a woman," Dad said.

"Strange," Mr. Kyle stated. "It's just strange. You'd think that some of us would know if a neighbor was doing some remodeling. As close of neighbors as we are, I mean. Well anyway, I thought I would ask you if I could borrow your air compressor? And I won't steal anything else while I'm in there!"

Dad and Mr. Kyle laughed. "No problem," Dad said. "I may need it back by the end of next week, though. I was hoping to install some paneling in the tack room of the barn. My other compressor isn't working."

"I should be through with it Monday or Tuesday," Mr. Kyle assured. "If you need it sooner, please call."

Dad followed Mr. Kyle to the shop and opened the big garage door. Mr. Kyle wheeled the compressor to his truck.

As Dad and Mr. Kyle talked about the price of colts this spring, Ben came walking around from the back of the barn, hitting two pipes together. "Clank, clank!" The sound echoed off the house. "Clank, clank!" The two men stopped their conversation and watched the approaching figure.

"Clenk, clenk!" came a new sound from just around the side of the barn. Then Matthew walked around the corner, hitting two smaller pipes together. "Clenk, clenk!"

"Hey, Andy, look at these neat pipes we found," Ben said, walking up to the boys. "They make all kinds of different sounds."

"We know," Andy said. "We were using these to help identify a sound."

"Well, it goes 'clank,'" Ben noted. "Except for Matthew's. His goes 'clenk.'"

"This must be your new son," Mr. Kyle smiled. "Hello there, Matthew, I'm Mr. Kyle. It's a pleasure to meet you."

Matthew got shy and hid behind Dad.

"He's just a little shy, yet," Dad said. "But let me tell you. He's getting the Nelson boy appetite!"

"That's great," Mr. Kyle praised. "Why before you know it, he'll be running his own detective agency around here." Then turning to Andy, he asked, "What was that you said, Andy? Trying to identify a sound or something? Is that another mystery you guys are working on?"

"Yes sir, it is. Actually, it's a sound we hear in the woods sometimes." Andy and Jason filled Mr. Kyle in on The Case of the Strange Bump.

Mr. Kyle got a gleam in his eyes, but only said, "Uh huh. Can you boys make that sound for me?"

"Well, it goes 'Bump . . . bump. . bump . bump, bump.'"

"I mean, can you make the sound using pipes? You said something about being able to make the same sound with pipes you had found?"

Jason ran and got the right pipe and skillfully made the sound. "Bump . . . bump. . bump . bump, bump."

"Perfect!" Mr. Kyle beamed. "You boys are pretty good, did you know that?"

"Do you know what could make a sound like

that?" Andy asked anxiously.

"Yes. It's a ruffed grouse, boys!"

"A bird? Are you sure?" Jason couldn't believe it. "I've never heard a bird make a sound like that before."

"Well, we don't have a lot of them around these parts. But I used to live in North Carolina before I moved here and we had them all the time," Mr. Kyle said.

"Why would they make a sound like that?" Ben asked.

"It is a mating call," Mr. Kyle informed. "The male is trying to attract a female ruffed grouse. And he does it by beating the air with his wings."

"That's neat!" exclaimed Andy. "Thanks a lot, Mr. Kyle. Jason, let's go look up 'ruffed grouse' in our books and learn more about them!"

The two older boys ran toward the house. Ben and Matthew seemed content to just keep banging the pipes together.

"Here it is," Jason exclaimed, holding an encyclopedia in his lap. "They are about fifteen inches tall and look sort of like a brown chicken with a black-banded tail and black folds on the sides of the neck. Look, they even took a picture of it beating its wings. It says here that in the spring, the male picks some special log and goes to it every day. He sits on it and makes that drumming sound. The sound can be heard for a great distance and may seem to be loud even though its a quarter of a mile away. That's probably why we got so confused as to where it was."

"Yes," Andy agreed. "What else does your book say?"

Midnight Sky

"Its range is from Alaska and northern Canada down to the Carolinas, and in the Appalachians to Georgia. Since our mountains are in the foothills of the Appalachian chain, I guess that's why we have a ruffed grouse too."

"It's one of the most prized game birds in North America," Andy read slowly from the bird book in his hands. "What does that mean?"

"It means that people hunt them. This book says that many of them are harvested by hunters, but that it doesn't seem to put them in danger of extinction. Also, they have lots of other enemies as well. They lay close to a dozen eggs at a time, but few ever make it to maturity because of their enemies."

"I wonder where they make their nests?" Andy asked. "Or where they stay during the day? If we knew, then we would have a better chance of seeing one."

Jason scanned his book. "It says here that their habitat is forests, especially if they have clearings scattered around. They usually make their nest at the foot of a tree. They also like overgrown pastures and abandoned farmland. I guess they need some cover, yet they have to be able to take off and fly if it's necessary."

"Here's something else neat. In the winter time they grow bristles on their toes, sort of like combs. They use them like snowshoes!" Andy thought that would be worth looking for, the next time it snowed.

"So, The Case of the Strange Bump is really and truly solved!" Andy enthused. "Wouldn't it be fun to see one actually make that sound? Why don't we try to see if we can find one and watch it?"

"It may be hard to do, but I'm willing to try," Jason assented. "Let's go!"

Try as they might, however, the boys were never able to see the ruffed grouse as it beat its wings. Still, it was exciting to know what was making that sound and why.

The rest of the day was spent helping Dad work around the farm. One of the mares was expecting a foal soon and the boys kept making trips to her stall to see if it had been born yet. Matthew got excited and kept pointing to the mare when they would look in on her. It was encouraging to see Matthew feel more and more comfortable at the Nelson farm.

After supper, the entire family took a walk through the woods. They were hoping to hear the ruffed grouse make his call, but they were almost through and still hadn't heard it.

"Listen," Dad said softly, causing everyone to stop walking. "There it is!"

Sure enough, the grouse was busily making his presence known. "Bump . . . bump. . bump . bump, bump."

"That's a bird making that sound," Dad said. "He does it like this." Dad demonstrated what he thought the grouse looked like. The fact that he puffed out his cheeks while beating the air with his arms was just too much for Ben. He broke out laughing and pointing at Dad. Soon everyone was laughing, even Matthew.

Ben tried to imitate Dad, but ended up looking like someone who had just drunk a gallon of water and was holding it all in his cheeks. His face got bright red. "Okay, Ben. You can breathe now," Mom instructed with a worried look. For some reason that caused everyone to laugh, even Dad.

When they got home, it was time for Bible. Dad read from the thirteenth chapter of Hebrews. "Remember them that are in bonds, as bound with them; and them which suffer adversity, as being yourselves also in the body," he reread verse three. "We all know that the verse is reminding us not to forget our brothers and sisters in Christ who are being persecuted. But it doesn't just say to remember them. It says that we are to remember them **as though we are also in bonds with them**. That's a lot stronger, isn't it? How can we do that?"

Everyone thought about it for a while. No one seemed to have a good answer to Dad's question at first. Finally, Jason offered a suggestion. "I think it means that we aren't supposed to just pray for them and then feel like we've done our part. We're supposed to keep them in our minds. We're supposed to try and see how they might be feeling right now."

"That's a good answer," Dad praised. "If we could just get half a sense of what it feels like to be really persecuted, I think our lives would be different. We would pray more, not just for those actually suffering, but for ourselves as well that we would remain faithful if we ever had to go through such persecution. We would be more grateful for what we do have. We would want to share our material blessings with those who are suffering. But I think Jason hit the nail on the head. We would try to realize how they are feeling."

"Sometimes they are happy," Ben noted.

"That's right," Dad agreed. "It has always been

amazing to me to read about those who are really suffering for Christ. We hear over and over the testimonies of persecuted Christians and how they really love those who are persecuting them. They get closer to God through the trial, not further away from Him. That would be something else good to reflect upon as we strive to 'remember them . . . as bound with them.'

"As we pray, let's ask God to help us to remember our brothers and sisters who are suffering as though we were right there with them. Let's ask God to show us exactly how we can do that, too." Everyone kneeled for prayer.

After prayer, Dad got out the hymn books and said, "I feel like singing. What would you like to sing tonight?"

"Number 585," Ben said, without even looking in his hymn book. *In the Garden* was his favorite hymn and he never got tired of singing it.

After several other songs, Dad announced, "Time for bed now, guys. Tomorrow will be here before you know it. Tomorrow's Sunday and we want to be fresh and ready to worship God with others."

"I hope it won't be too long before we get to go with Dad to the building supply store," Jason commented as the boys lay down in their beds. "Maybe the Case of the Missing Tools will finally be solved!"

Andy was not as enthusiastic. He remembered how the lady at the checkout hadn't been all that helpful. Maybe, even with their piece of wood, the clerk wouldn't be able to match it. Or maybe he would match it, but refuse to tell them who had purchased it. Somehow Andy felt that the people at the store knew more than they were willing to tell about the tools. Rather than share all of these doubts and concerns, however, he simply answered, "Maybe."

Chapter Twenty-two

On Monday, when Dad got home from work, he loaded up the boys and headed to the building supply store. He walked back to the paint department and waited for someone to come and help him. A young man, probably not more than 18 or 19, walked up. "Can I help you?"

"Maybe," Dad said. "I have this little chip of wood that has some paint on it. I feel pretty sure that the paint on it was mixed here. Can you tell me what color it is?"

"No problem!" the clerk answered. "Forgot, did you? Well, that's okay, everybody does." Dad was about to correct the clerk by telling him the facts of the case, but the clerk continued talking. He was one of those clerks that seems to love to talk non-stop. "We'll just put it here on this little thing. Okay. Now we turn this on. See, it's scanning the surface of the wood to determine what the color is. Can you see how it's doing it, boys? Pretty soon. Yes, here it is now." He looked at a screen. "Let's see...Midnight Sky. That's the name of the color of blue on the wood chip. See how easy that was? Took only a few seconds, huh? This modern technology is amazing! Here's the exact mix directions we need to mix you another gallon. Or did you just need a quart?"

Dad didn't know how to begin. "I don't need a quart or a gallon. I was going to tell you that I was curious to know the color, although I wasn't going to buy any."

"Oh!" the clerk said in amazement. "That's a new one on me. Do you collect colored wood chips?" he said, trying to make a joke.

"No," Dad replied. "Actually, here's what has happened . . ." Then Dad proceeded to tell him the whole story of the Case of the Missing Tools. When Dad mentioned the police, the clerk got a serious look on his face. Finally, Dad concluded, "So you see, now that we know the color and the date that the paint was purchased, we were hoping that you could tell us who it was that bought the paint. You certainly don't have to, if you don't want to, however."

The clerk laughed nervously. "Our computer stores information about paint colors by the customer's name. So if you came in and told me your name, I could look up any colors that have been mixed for you. But since the information is in there some-where, let's see if I can figure out how to retrieve it." He played with the keyboard a while and watched the results on the screen. "No, that won't let me do it. . . And that says we need a zip code . . . Let's see what happens if I choose this icon . . . Hey, look at that! It's giving me a screen of people who have bought Midnight Sky blue paint. I didn't know that was such a popular color. . . Let's see, what date was it again?"

Dad repeated the date to the man. Jason and Andy were so excited they were about to shout. However, they tried to look very dignified. Ben had gotten restless and was walking down the aisle absently tapping paint cans with a paint stirrer. "Ben, please don't do that," Dad corrected.

"Okay, with that date . . . yes, here it is . . . the

lady's name is . . . well it's not a lady's name after all!" The clerk, who must have been a drama student, kept their suspense as long as he could, then finally said, "The mysterious customer is Jonathan Beavers."

"Uncle John!" shouted Jason and Andy in unison.

"Boys, don't shout in the store," Dad corrected.

"We're sorry, Dad. But how can it be Uncle John?" asked Andy. "Wouldn't he have told you he was borrowing the tools? And why did the note have a lady's handwriting on it?

Dad was just as confused as the boys were. "I have no idea. I'll find out, though."

Dad thanked the clerk very much for his assistance. The clerk went whistling down the aisle to help another customer.

When they were in the car, Andy started laughing. "What are you laughing at, Andy?" questioned Jason.

"I was just thinking," Andy replied, still laughing. "Wouldn't it have been funny if Uncle John had been arrested for borrowing Dad's tools?"

Even Dad laughed at that. "I just can't picture Uncle John standing in front of those tall rulers at the police station getting his mug shot taken! I don't think Aunt Sue would ever get over it!"

"That was really neat the way the clerk was able to find out the name of our paint color, wasn't it?" Jason reflected. "Midnight Sky isn't a name of a color that I would have just guessed. I wonder why they would name a color a funny name like that?"

"I suppose paint companies want to have different names for their colors, so that people will remember them better. And they try to make their shades a little different from every other company, so that once you buy their paint, you have to buy more from them, and not from a competitor." Dad smiled at Jason in the rear view mirror. "You might want to think about that if you become a big paint company president some-day." Jason just grinned back at Dad.

When they got home, the boys couldn't wait to tell Mom the news. However, she was rocking baby Leah to sleep. "I'll going to call Uncle John, and fill him in on our mystery." Dad said. "I'm sure he'll enjoy learning about it. Why don't you boys help Cathy finish the dishes and sweep up?"

Before long, Dad returned to the kitchen. "Well, I can now fill you in on all of the details of the case that are still a little fuzzy to you."

Even Cathy stopped cleaning to listen. The boys had filled her in on what they knew and she was anxious to learn more.

Before Dad could begin, Mom walked into the kitchen, stretching her neck to the left and blinking a little from the bright lights. "Leah finally went to sleep. I must have dozed off in the rocking chair, myself."

"We'll try to keep the noise down," Dad offered. "Anyway, it seems that Uncle John did ask permission to use my tools."

"Honestly, Dad, he didn't ask me," Jason said.

"Me either," Andy echoed.

"I didn't talk to Uncle John," Cathy added, trying to be of help.

"I can't even remember talking to Uncle John," piped in Ben.

Dad looked at Mom, smiling. "Sure, I told him it

was okay to borrow your tools," Mom admitted. "I didn't think I was doing anything wrong."

"You weren't!" Dad said. "Not at all. It's just that no one knew Uncle John was borrowing them and we thought that . . . that is, we thought they had been stolen."

"Timothy, are you serious?" Mom asked, laughing. "Why, I told John right before our trip to Russia that he could use your tools. He was going to install some hardwood floors and put up some new trim in their den. He's used your tools before and you said he always takes good care of them."

"I know, honey," Dad said, giving Mom a hug. "But no one knew that but you."

"Why didn't someone ask me?" she questioned.

Dad looked at the boys who looked back at him. "I don't know," Dad laughed. "We've talked about it, but maybe . . ." He thought some more. "You know, I don't think you've ever been in the room while we've discussed it. Boys, can you remember?"

Jason and Andy thought. Finally, Jason agreed, "I can't remember ever talking about it when Mom was around. It wasn't a secret."

Mom laughed. "I've been so preoccupied with Leah and Matthew that I might not have really been listening to your conversations, anyway. I'm sorry."

"It's no problem," Dad reassured her. The boys and Dad tried to remember all the times they had discussed the case, and came to the conclusion that Mom had never been present.

"Why was it a lady's handwriting?" asked Jason, wanting to get some of the facts of the case straightened out in his mind.

Midnight Sky

Dad explained the note on the air compressor to Mom. "Uncle John tried to return some of the tools while we were still in Russia. Since you guys had locked the shop up and taken away the key he had to take them back home again. Then when he was through using all of them, he asked Aunt Sue to drop them by the house. That was after we had returned from our trip to Russia. Since none of us were home, Aunt Sue had to unload them herself."

"I hope they weren't heavy," Mom said sympathetically.

"The air compressor is heavy, but it's on wheels. Anyway, she was able to drag the compressor into the shop and barely got the chop saw on the bench. After she had everything in the shop she decided to leave a note thanking us for the tools, since we were gone. She didn't write more than "Thank you" because she thought that we knew who had borrowed them. She didn't have any paper in her purse and had to tear off the back of an old calendar to write the note."

"The Case of the Missing Tools is really and truly solved!" Andy exclaimed.

"Yes," Dad agreed. "And even though we would have eventually learned the facts of the case, we were able to solve it sooner thanks to the efforts of The Great Detective Agency. Thanks, guys!"

"We're always ready to help," Jason reminded, making an entry in his spiral notebook and then closing it. "Call on us anytime!" With that the partners of The Great Detective Agency put their notebooks in their back pockets and walked cheerfully out of the room.

The End

A Note From the Authors

In *Midnight Sky* you have read of a special ministry called the Voice of the Martyrs. This ministry provides Bibles, food, clothing, and other help to Christians around the world who are persecuted for their faith. A prayer calendar, books, free homeschool study materials (called LINK International), and further information are available from: Voice of the Martyrs, P.O. Box 443, Bartlesville, OK 74005; (800) 747-0085. Their email address is vomusa@aol.com.

Our primary goal in publishing is to provide wholesome books in a manner that brings honor to our Lord Jesus Christ. In the next several pages you can learn more about the books we offer. We always welcome your comments, suggestions, and most importantly, your prayers. If you would like to contact us, you can reach us at this address:

Mr. and Mrs. Stephen B. Castleberry
Castleberry Farms Press
P.O. Box 337
Poplar, WI 54864

Castleberry Farms Press

Our primary goal in publishing is to provide wholesome books in a manner that brings honor to our Lord. We believe in setting no evil thing before our eyes (Psalm 101:3) and although there are many outstanding books, we have had trouble finding enough good reading material for our children. Therefore, we feel the Lord has led us to start this family business.

We believe the following: The Bible is the infallible true Word of God. That God is the Creator and Controller of the universe. That Jesus Christ is the only begotten Son of God, born of the virgin Mary, lived a perfect life, was crucified, buried, rose again, sits at the right hand of God, and makes intercession for the saints. That Jesus Christ is the only Savior and way to the Father. That salvation is based on faith alone, but true faith will produce good works. That the Holy Spirit is given to believers as Guide and Comforter. That the Lord Jesus will return again. That man was created to glorify God and enjoy Him forever.

We began writing and publishing in mid-1996 and hope to add more books in the future if the Lord is willing. All books are written by Mr. and Mrs. Castleberry.

The Courtship Series

These books are written to encourage those who intend to follow a Biblically-based courtship that includes the active involvement of parents. The main characters are committed followers of Jesus Christ, and Christian family values are emphasized throughout. The reader will be encouraged to heed parental advice and to live in obedience to the Lord.

NEW! *Jeff McLean: His Courtship*

Follow the story of Jeff McLean as he seeks God's direction for his life. This book is the newest in our courtship series, and is written from a young man's perspective. A discussion of godly traits to seek in young men and women is included as part of the story. February 1998. Paperback. $7.50 (plus shipping and handling).

The Courtship of Sarah McLean

Sarah McLean is a nineteen year-old girl who longs to become a wife and mother. The book chronicles a period of two years, in which she has to learn to trust her parents and God fully in their decisions for her future. Paperback, 2nd printing, 1997. $7.50 (plus shipping and handling).

Waiting for Her Isaac

Sixteen year-old Beth Grant is quite happy with her life and has no desire for any changes. But God has many lessons in store before she is ready for courtship. The story of Beth's spiritual journey toward godly womanhood is told along with the story of her courtship. Paperback. 1997. $7.50 (plus shipping and handling).

The Farm Mystery Series

Join Jason and Andy as they try to solve the mysterious happenings on the Nelson family's farm. These are books that the whole family will enjoy. In fact, many have used them as read-aloud-to-the-family books. Parents can be assured that there are no murders or other objectionable elements in these books. The boys learn lessons in obedience and responsibility while having lots of fun. There are no worldly situations or language, and no boy-girl relationships. Just happy and wholesome Christian family life, with lots of everyday adventure woven in.

Footprints in the Barn

Who is the man in the green car? What is going on in the hayloft? Is there something wrong with the mailbox? And what's for lunch? The answers to these and many other interesting questions are found in the book <u>Footprints in the Barn</u>. Hardcover. 1996. $12 (plus shipping and handling).

The Mysterious Message

The Great Detective Agency is at it once again, solving mysteries on the Nelson farmstead. Why is there a pile of rocks in the woods? Is someone stealing gas from the mill? How could a railroad disappear? And will Jason and Andy have to eat biscuits without honey? You will have to read this second book in the Farm Mystery Series to find out. Paperback. 1997. $7.50 (plus shipping and handling).

NEW: Midnight Sky

What is that sound in the woods? Has someone been stealing Dad's tools? Why is a strange dog barking at midnight? And will the Nelsons be able to adopt Russian children? <u>Midnight Sky</u> provides the answers. Paperback. 1998. $7.50 (plus shipping and handling).

Other Books

Our Homestead Story: The First Years

The true and humorous account of one family's journey toward a more self-sufficient life-style with the help of God. Read about our experiences with cows, chickens, horses, sheep, gardening and more. Paperback. 1996. $7.50 (plus shipping and handling).

COMING SOON
The Orchard Lane Series:
In the Spring of the Year

Meet the Hunter family and share in their lives as they move to a new home. The first in our newest series, <u>In the Spring of the Year</u> is written especially for children ages 5-10. Nancy, Caleb, and Emily learn about obedience and self-denial while enjoying the simple pleasures of innocent childhood. Please write for details about pricing and availability. Hopefully it will be ready in May, 1998.

Shipping and Handling Costs

The shipping and handling charge is $2.00 for the first book and 50¢ for each additional book you buy in the same order.

You can save on shipping by getting an order together with your friends or homeschool group. On orders of 10-24 books, shipping is only 50¢ per book. Orders of 25 or more books are shipped FREE. Just have each person write a check for their own total, send in all the checks, and indicate **one** address for shipping.

To order, please send a check for the total, including shipping (Wisconsin residents, please add 5.5% sales tax on the total, including shipping and handling charges) to:

Castleberry Farms Press
Dept. MS
P.O. Box 337
Poplar, WI 54864

Please note that prices are subject to change.